'Oh, for pity's sake, give up the innocent act, Roy. Your cover's blown. I know you're nothing but a gigolo.'

'A gigolo,' he repeated in such a numbed voice that Kate had a momentary pang of doubt.

The doubt grew while he continued to stare. But gradually the startled look in his eyes cleared and he cocked his head on one side, looking at her with a type of interested curiosity. Then suddenly, he laughed.

Dear Reader

In February, we celebrate one of the most romantic times of the year—St Valentine's Day, when messages of true love are exchanged. At Mills & Boon we feel that our novels carry the Valentine spirit on throughout the year and we hope that readers agree. Dipping into the pages of our books will give you a taste of true romance every month...so chase away those winter blues and look forward to spring with Mills & Boon!

Till next month,

The Editor

Miranda Lee is Australian, living near Sydney. Born and raised in the bush, she was boarding-school educated and briefly pursued a classical music career before moving to Sydney and embracing the world of computers. Happily married, with three daughters, she began writing when family commitments kept her at home. She likes to create stories that are believable, modern, fast-paced and sexy. Her interests include reading meaty sagas, doing word puzzles, gambling and going to the movies.

Recent titles by the same author:

SIMPLY IRRESISTIBLE
MARRIAGE IN JEOPARDY
MISTRESS OF DECEPTION

HEART-THROB
FOR HIRE

BY
MIRANDA LEE

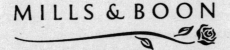

MILLS & BOON LIMITED
ETON HOUSE, 18-24 PARADISE ROAD
RICHMOND, SURREY TW9 1SR

*First published in Great Britain 1993
by Mills & Boon Limited*

© Miranda Lee 1993

*Australian copyright 1993
Philippine copyright 1994
This edition 1994*

ISBN 0 263 78388 X

*Set in Times Roman 10½ on 12 pt.
01-9402-50880 C*

Made and printed in Great Britain

CHAPTER ONE

KATE was early for work. *Very* early for work. There again, she was very early for work every day. Investment executives who wanted to go places at International Credit and Finance started early and finished late. They lived and breathed ICAF. They had no time for anything else. Not if they were truly ambitious.

And Kate was truly ambitious. *Wasn't she?*

Dismissing this niggling thought after a moment's doubt, she swept through her office door, the one with KATE REYNOLDS—FOREIGN INVESTMENTS in gold lettering. Her secretary's desk outside was empty, and would remain so for another hour. Estelle's starting time was eight-thirty, and, like all normal girls, she didn't show her face till thirty seconds before she had to.

Normal girls?

Kate frowned as she closed the door. *Now* what am I implying about myself? she worried. That I'm *not* normal?

Well, most *normal* females of thirty were either married, or mothers, or both, she reminded herself truthfully. The rest had boyfriends or fiancés or live-in lovers or *de facto* husbands or *something!* They didn't go home every night to an empty bed, a good book and a canary for company. And if they did, they certainly didn't *like* it.

But *she* did.

5

Did that mean she wasn't normal?

Certainly not. There had to be many women in this world who chose spinsterhood and celibacy as a life-style. It was nothing to be defensive about. Besides, it was *her* life and if she didn't want to spend it with a man, then that was her business and no one else's.

Kate placed her black leather briefcase neatly beside her desk, hooked her umbrella over the corner coat-stand, then turned to open the vertical blinds that ran along the huge window behind her swivel-based chair.

Sunlight flooded in as the slats parted then slid back, revealing a magnificent view across the street to the botanical gardens. Kate was glad to see that the overnight rain looked like clearing away. Weather and appointments permitting, she liked to eat her lunch in those gardens, usually on the bench under the big plane tree. Her eyes went to that bench now and what she saw drew a gasp of alarm.

A man—probably an old wino—was lying on that bench, apparently asleep, and two suspicious-looking teenagers were sneaking up on him.

'Oh, my God!' Kate cried out in horror when she saw the young thugs pounce. She watched with heart pounding as a wild scuffle erupted, the old wino doing surprisingly well till one of his attackers hit him with something. He staggered, then fell, clutching his head.

Kate didn't stop to think. Snatching up her um-brella, she raced through the still deserted offices, down the stairwell and out through the foyer of the building, bursting through the glass doors and across the road with scant concern for the blessedly light traffic. Nevertheless, one taxi had to brake hard to miss her, the driver giving her a piece of his mind through the open window.

But she ignored the curses and lunged onwards across Macquarie Street, oblivious of everything but the driving need to help that poor old man. Perhaps she should have stopped to think what a five-foot-four, fifty-two-kilo female could do against a couple of thugs. Thinking, however, was not on her agenda at the moment. She had been fired to action by a fierce fury at the incident she had just witnessed.

'Stop that, you rotten mongrels!' she screamed as she raced through the park entrance, bringing several weird stares from passers-by. But they couldn't see what she had seen from street level. There were too many bushes and trees along the fence that bordered the gardens.

By the time she had the plane tree in sight, the thugs had their victim on the ground and were kicking him.

'Police! Police! Over here!' Kate yelled at the top of her voice.

Both of the assailants stopped what they were doing and looked up, startled either by her screams or the manic quality of her approach. Only later was Kate to realise that some of her frizzy red hair had come loose from its prim knot to fly about her face so that she looked like some Irish witch. She was also brandishing her umbrella like King Henry going into battle.

Whatever, the two attackers fled, leaving her alone with the vagrant, who was still curled up on the ground, clutching his stomach.

'Are . . . are you all right?' she asked breathlessly.

When he tipped back his head to grimace up at her, she couldn't help staring. For he was not at all old. Not even remotely. And while his black waves were tangled, his blue eyes bloodshot and his chin sprouting a three-day growth, he didn't look like a vagrant or

a wino either. There was something far too sharp
behind that piercing blue gaze.

'I've felt better,' he grunted.

'Oh!' she gasped when she saw blood trickling down
his forehead. 'You're bleeding!' And she fell to her
knees beside him, dropping her umbrella on the grass
while her hands fluttered helplessly.

He glanced down over his body. 'Where?'

'Your...your head.'

'Aah...' He patted it gingerly, his fingers quickly
staining with fresh blood. 'Got a hanky?' he asked,
another grimace on his face.

A surprisingly attractive face, she thought with
some confusion. Who would have believed an unshaven, bleary-eyed face could be so *attractive*? It
wasn't as though it was even handsome under the dark
stubble. Why, it was all hard angles and planes. His
nose looked as if it might have been broken once or
twice as well.

Yet she found herself staring at that face for several
seconds before dragging her attention back to his
question. 'Oh—er—um—no. But I could—er—ask
someone, I suppose.' She glanced around, but the only
person passing near by was a fast-striding businessman
who clearly didn't want to become involved.

'No, don't bother,' she was told. And without
blinking an eyelid he ripped the left sleeve out of his
tracksuit, rolling it up and pressing the soft ball against
the wound.

Kate stared at his bare arm with the same kind of
reaction she'd had to his unexpectedly attractive face.
Once again, her response startled her, for she was not
a girl to have ever been impressed by a muscular limb.
Or a muscular anything! Right from childhood, she

had been trained to appreciate brainpower, not brawn. Yet here she was, gawking at this man's bulging biceps.

An embarrassed blush flooded her cheeks. Luckily, the reason for her embarrassment wasn't looking at her now. He was trying to get to his feet. Not altogether successfully.

Kate really had no option but to help him.

Gathering herself, she gripped him by the upper arms and hauled upwards.

Lord, but he was so heavy. And so *tall*! Her mouth must have rounded as his body slowly unfolded ever upwards, her stunned green eyes lifting to wryly amused blue ones.

'I haven't thanked you,' he said in a voice as deep as his chest. 'You're one hell of a brave lady. Or one hell of a fool,' he added wryly. 'Which one is it?'

'Fool, I think,' she muttered with a degree of self-mockery. For here she was, a highly intelligent thirty-year-old career woman, letting a well built giant of no older than twenty-five throw her for a loop. It was not only mortifying but mystifying. He wasn't her type at all.

Come, now, you don't *have* a type, inserted the dry voice of honesty.

The sight of fresh blood seeping out from under the sleeve compress brought her sharply back to the problem at hand. 'You must come up to my office,' she said briskly. 'It's just across the road. I can call you a doctor. That cut will need stitching.'

His dark brows beetled together in a frown. 'But that's a lot of trouble for you. You've been kind enough as it is, coming to my rescue the way you did.

I can just as easily catch a taxi to a hospital and have myself seen to.'

'And spend endless hours in Casualty waiting to be seen? I wouldn't wish that on a dog!'

She flushed when she realised how that sounded. There again, this chap wasn't exactly the cream of the crop. OK, so maybe he wasn't the meths-drinking vagrant she'd originally thought he was, but his appearance still left a lot to be desired. His black tracksuit looked as if it had been dragged out of a charity bin—what was left of it, that was. As for his trainers... Several large dogs had obviously been using them for a tug-of-war.

If clothes maketh the man, then this individual was in big trouble, she was thinking as her eyes travelled slowly over him.

He'd look pretty good *without* clothes, though, came the sudden and highly uncharacteristic thought.

Shocked by it, her eyes snapped guiltily up to his, only to find him looking at her with a curious expression on his face.

'How old are you?' he asked abruptly.

It took her somewhat aback. 'Thirty. Why?'

'Thirty,' he muttered under his breath. 'Not blonde, either. Man must be going mad. Knew it had been too long...'

'What *are* you muttering about?' Kate demanded, growing impatient both with him and herself.

'Nothing,' he mumbled, and shook his head.

'Well, are you coming with me or not?'

He suddenly swayed on his feet, his colour not at all good.

'Look, you're definitely coming with me and that's that!' Kate ordered, and, firmly taking his right arm, began to propel him forward.

'Yes, ma'am. Whatever you say, ma'am. You're the boss.'

'You *are* the boss, aren't you?' he repeated after she had safely deposited him on the chesterfield in her office and returned to her desk.

Kate looked up from where she was already dialling the company doctor. 'Only of my division,' she returned, waving him silent while she made the call.

'The doctor will be here shortly,' she was happy to relay one minute later. 'I caught him just before he left home on his morning rounds. Right,' she went on efficiently, 'do you want me to call the police as well?'

'God, no. I couldn't stand the hassle. I'm too damned tired. They wouldn't find those kids anyway.'

'Why do you think they attacked you?'

He shrugged. 'Who knows? They were probably junkies, looking for money.'

'On *you*?'

He smiled at her expression of disbelief.

'You really shouldn't judge a book by its cover, you know. I'm not as poorly off as I look.'

'In that case what on earth were you doing spending the night on a park bench?'

'I didn't spend the night. I was merely having a rest.'

'A rest? From what?'

'I was jogging when this dizzy spell suddenly struck. I had a late night the night before, you see. I—er—um…' He hesitated, then shrugged again. 'It was just a late night.' Clearly he didn't want to tell her what he had really been doing. Several scenarios entered her mind. Breaking and entering at Bondi; drug deals on some seedy Paddington corner; pimping up at the Cross. He fitted every one of them.

Yet some weird feminine intuition Kate didn't know she had reassured her that this chap was not really a dangerous individual. Not in any criminal sense. His danger—if one could call it that—lay in his overt virility. Sex appeal fairly oozed out of every pore. Kate imagined most women would be affected by it. Yet her own response was still irritating. She would have thought she wasn't most women.

'You don't have to explain,' she said curtly. 'Can I get you a drink? You're looking pale.'

'Am I? Well, yes, I'd appreciate a drink.'

'What would you like?'

'What can I have?'

His smile was decidedly cheeky, and incredibly engaging. Kate had to stop herself from smiling fatuously back.

'Anything within reason,' was her crisp reply.

'How about good old H_2O?'

'Coming right up.'

Kate felt his eyes on her as she walked across the room towards her private washroom. Yes, she thought quite savagely. He was one of those men who liked looking at women, who would enjoy just sitting in a park and watching them walk by. His eyes would zero in on their breasts, or legs, or bottom, and soon he would be undressing them with his eyes.

Was he doing that to her now? Wondering what she might look like, naked, in his bed?

She was certain he wasn't. And that certainty was accompanied by a rather telling dismay. What was the matter with her today? First, she'd started doubting the choices she had made in life, both career-wise and personally. And now...now she was wanting some ne'er-do-well to lust after her.

What was she trying to prove to herself? That she could have a man if she really wanted one? That there *was* a desirable woman somewhere underneath the sexless suits she wore to work?

Stifling a groan, she resisted hurrying those last couple of steps before she could turn the corner of the washroom and so be out of sight of those knowing blue eyes. Instead, she did, if anything, walk even slower, hating herself for the small sway that crept into her hips, but seemingly unable to stop herself from sending out that silent sexual message.

Kate *did* groan when the washroom mirror revealed the state of her hair. She looked like a witch!

The sight of her wayward tresses, plus her pale, freckled face, certainly brought her back down to earth.

You're still plain, darling, she reminded herself brutally. You've always been plain. OK, so you've dispensed with the heavy glasses. And you've finally had your teeth fixed. But you're still plain. Besides which, it's too late. Too, too late.

Why, if that man out there made a pass at you, you'd die of fright. Yes, fright. You're a coward, sweetheart. So crawl back into your safe little cocoon, coward, and don't for pity's sake, try to be sexy. It's pathetic. Really pathetic.

Chastened, she swiftly stuffed the wayward tresses back into the topknot, dropping her eyes from her reflection while she filled one of the clean glasses on the shelf with water.

But before she could turn away from the vanity mirror, she found herself glancing at herself one more time, and still stupidly wishing she hadn't worn her navy serge suit that morning. It was more severely tailored than her other suits, bordering on mannish with its double-breasted blazer-style jacket and straight-legged trousers. Teamed as it was today with a crisp white shirt, she looked like the classic clichéd woman executive. In short, like a feminist superbitch.

Suddenly, her self-critical thoughts infuriated her. Truly, Kate, you're being ridiculous, she told herself sharply. Prior to today, you've been very happy with your life. Very happy indeed. The sooner you get that macho bum out of your office, the better.

'Here you are,' she said with controlled civility on returning, pressing the glass into his left hand. It was, she noted ruefully, as big and male-looking as the rest of him.

Stepping back, she folded her arms and watched him drink before saying coolly, 'Do you realise I don't know your name?'

His smile was odd. 'Yes, I do.'

The slight smugness behind his answer threw her for a second. What was he, an incorrigible smart alec? 'Well, what is it?' she almost snapped.

'Roy.'

'Roy what?'

'Roy...Fitzsimmons,' he added after a slight hesitation and a speculative glance at her.

She frowned. Was that name supposed to mean something to her? It didn't. Not in the slightest.

He seemed highly satisfied by her lack of recognition.

'And yours is Kate,' he went on before she could ask him if she was supposed to recognise his name. 'Kate Reynolds.'

Surprise made her stare at him.

He grinned. 'It's on your office door.'

'Oh... oh, yes, of course. Silly of me.'

'I doubt you would ever be silly, Miss Reynolds. It *is* Miss, isn't it? Or is it Ms?'

His drily amused tone annoyed her. But she refused to show any annoyance, giving him the blandest of looks. 'Miss or Ms. I have no real preference. After all, they both mean the same thing.'

'Which is?'

'I'm not married. I don't even have a boyfriend.'

Now why did she have to add that? It sounded as if she wanted him to know that she was free and un-attached, which wasn't true. *Was* it?

Good lord, she'd already been through that merry-go-round in her mind.

'Neither do I,' he agreed. 'A girlfriend, that is,' he added with an amused twinkle in his eyes. 'I guess a chap has to make such matters clear these days, since it's not unheard-of for a man to openly have a boy-friend. Still, let me assure you, Kate—I can call you Kate, can't I?—that I am not that sort of man.'

She had never doubted it. What she did doubt was what this fellow's game was. Did he honestly think she believed this sudden charm was for *her*? That he was interested in her as a woman?

The doctor's arrival at that point was extremely welcome. Kate could feel herself becoming increas-ingly rattled by this Roy fellow. She was glad to re-treat behind her desk while the doctor examined, then stitched up the two-inch gash. By the time he left, she had herself fully under control again. Yet when Roy said his goodbyes and stood up to leave, she could hardly contain a sigh of relief.

But he hesitated at the door, glancing back over his shoulder at her. 'I don't feel I've thanked you properly,' he said. 'How about I take you out to dinner tonight in appreciation?'

Kate's heart leapt. My God, he was asking her out!

But no sooner had the flattering elation swept in than reality returned. And suspicion. *Why* was he asking her out? Was it really gratitude or did he have some other devious motive?

It came to her then that he might be one of those men who preyed on rich older women. She'd noticed the way he'd looked around her elegantly furnished office, as though he was quite impressed. Maybe he thought if he took her out, gave her a bit of slap and tickle, she would be oh, so grateful. Maybe his late night last night had been spent in some wealthy widow's bed.

A feeling of revulsion sent a shiver down her spine.

'Thank you for the offer, Roy,' she returned rather frostily, 'but that's really not necessary. I would have done the same for anyone.'

There! If he didn't get the hint he was as thick as a brick. She was not bowled over by his macho appeal. At least, not so much that her common sense had flown out the window. She knew what she was, and she wasn't the sort of girl this sort of man would look twice at. Obviously he had to have some ulterior motive for asking her out.

His expression was disgruntled, confirming her belief that he had had some scam in mind. Maybe, after dinner, he would just happen to discover he'd forgotten his wallet so that she had to pay. She'd heard of such men. Con men. Amateur gigolos, taking advantage of the loneliness in the lives of women like herself. They stopped at nothing in their quest for the quick and easy dollar. Why, they were even prepared to go to bed with their prey, no matter how old or plain they were, if there was a buck at the end of it.

The unwanted image of Roy standing beside her bed, slowly taking his clothes off, sent a flush of embarrassing heat up her neck and into her cheeks.

'I'd still like to take you out,' he persisted. 'Are you busy tonight, is that it? What about tomorrow night?'

Now she was really rattled. For she was sorely tempted to go out with him and to hell with common sense. How nice it would be to be seen in the company of such a young, overpoweringly sexy man! How flattering to her undernourished female ego.

How demeaning, don't you mean? that horrid voice piped up again. Do you think everyone won't know what he's up to? Or what you want from him?

Again she shuddered, the reaction this time bringing a small frown from Roy's wide, masculine forehead.

'I'm sorry, Roy,' she said swiftly. 'But the truth is I just don't go out with men.'

The look on his face made her want the ground to open up and swallow her. For of course she didn't mean what he thought she meant.

'I see,' he said slowly, his expression one of understated shock.

'I'm sorry,' she muttered again, her cheeks burning. But perhaps it was best if he did think she was gay. Then he wouldn't keep pestering her for a date.

CHAPTER TWO

THE red roses were delivered the following morning to Estelle's desk, shortly after ten. She fairly burst into Kate's office with them, showing both surprise and avid curiosity.

'They're for *you*!' she exclaimed, eyes disbelieving.

Kate knew immediately who had sent them, the realisation shooting an involuntary shiver of pleasure through her. Outwardly, however, she maintained her usual composure.

'How nice,' she said calmly. 'I dare say they're from Roy,' she added before Estelle started making speculations about the men at work. Not that any of them had shown any interest in her during her three years at the company.

'Roy who?'

Kate was neither surprised nor annoyed by the blunt question. Estelle had been her secretary since her promotion a year ago, and though the girl had a hide as thick as an elephant—or perhaps because of it—a relaxed camaraderie had sprung up between the two women. Really, it had been a case of either tolerate the girl's forthright ways or fire her, which was rather drastic since she was a good worker when she was actually in the office. A scatter-brain, though, where men were concerned.

'Fitzsimmons, I think he said his last name was,' Kate told her. 'I gave him a helping hand with something yesterday and I dare say this is his way of saying thank you.

Perhaps you'd like to bring them over to me, Estelle?'
she went on with wry amusement at her secretary's
stunned state. 'That way I can read the attached note.'

Estelle lurched across the room, handing over the roses
with her mouth still gaping. It snapped shut then burst
open. 'You can't mean *the* Roy Fitzsimmons was in this
office yesterday. Oh, Kate, tell me that's not so! I'll die
if that was so and I missed him.'

Kate placed the beautiful blooms carefully down on
her desk, glancing up at Estelle's anguished face with a
frown on her own. She remembered how Roy had been
surprised that she didn't recognise his name. It dawned
on her then that he must be some kind of celebrity, the
thought bringing a certain relief. There she'd been
thinking he was a layabout, and all along he was someone
quite famous.

'You know, I thought I recognised his name at the
time,' she lied outrageously, 'but I couldn't quite put my
finger on it. Who exactly *is* Roy Fitzsimmons, anyway?'

Estelle stared at her boss as though she were a little
green man from Mars. 'Honestly, Kate, you mean you
don't *know*? Lord, where have you been all your life?
Roy Fitzsimmons would have to be the most well known
footballer in the whole of Australia, not to mention the
most gorgeous! A couple of years ago he starred in one
of those calendars that feature macho types. He was one
of the hunks of the month. I used to have his picture
on my bedroom wall, but I recently replaced it with
James Dean. I'm into James Dean these days.'

Estelle was into anything that wore trousers, Kate
thought drily. But what of her revelations about Roy?

Kate couldn't deny feeling a little silly about not
recognising the man yesterday. But really, sport had never
interested her. Oh, she liked watching the Olympic

Games, but that was more patriotism than a love of physical competition. During her school years, she'd spent every sports afternoon in the library.

'When exactly was he in here?' Estelle went on in an aggrieved tone. 'Why didn't I see him?'

'It was before you arrived in the morning.'

'Before I arrived?' She looked puzzled. 'What was he doing in here so early?'

'He'd—er—fallen over and cut his head while jogging in the park. I saw the accident happen and brought him up here so that a doctor could have a look at him.'

'Have a look at him . . .' Estelle's groan was tortured. 'What I wouldn't give for a look at that gorgeous body up close! And there you were, not even recognising him!'

Kate shrugged helplessly, then bent to sniff the roses. There was very little scent, which was a shame, she thought. But they were indeed still beautiful. With slightly shaking fingers she slipped the note out of the attached envelope and started to read silently.

'Oh, don't be a meanie!' the secretary exclaimed. 'Tell me what it says!'

Kate's nervous laugh might have been revealing if Estelle was that sort of girl. But she was not the intuitive type. 'Truly, Estelle, it's quite impersonal. Just, "Thank you again, Kate." Signed "Roy".'

She didn't add the PS which said, *I still want to take you out to dinner in appreciation. If you change your mind, here's my phone number.*

Kate closed the note and slipped it into her top desk drawer, giving her goggle-eyed secretary the benefit of a distracting smile. 'Perhaps you could rustle up a vase for these?' And she handed the red roses back.

The girl hesitated, as though unwilling to let this conversation go. But then she sighed, shrugged and made her way resignedly out of the office, shutting the door behind her.

Kate immediately jumped to her feet, giving in to the feeling of elation and excitement she'd been trying to dampen down since she'd read that postscript. He still wanted to take her out. He was not a bum. He couldn't possibly be after her money.

Of course . . . given the new set of circumstances, the dinner offer undoubtedly *was* just gratitude. Since he thought she was gay, it couldn't really be anything else.

Maybe, though, if she enlightened him about her sexuality, told him he had misunderstood . . .

No! she told herself harshly. Stop being ridiculous!

Her elation died, replaced by stark reality. A man like that would have women falling all over themselves to get to him. Just look at Estelle's reaction.

Why would he ever be interested in *you*? came the savage thought. A thirty-year-old, very ordinary-looking career woman! And why, of all the men in the world, are you interested in *him*?

He's too young. He's not intellectually inclined. He is, to all intents and purposes, the last male you should be attracted to and the very last you would have a chance of winning.

And yet she *was* attracted to him. She very definitely was. And he had given her his phone number. All she had to do to see him again was find the courage to dial, to say yes. Why shouldn't she at least have that pleasure for herself? One miserable little evening of his company. Besides, she *would* like him to know that she was heterosexual. Pride demanded it.

When Estelle returned with the roses in a large glass vase, Kate was standing at her window, blindly looking down at the traffic, gnawing at her bottom lip.

'Where would you like me to put these?' the girl asked.

'Just put them on my desk, will you?'

'They *are* lovely, aren't they?'

'Yes,' Kate agreed, then turned to look at them. 'Yes, they are.'

'I still can't get over Roy Fitzsimmons being in this very office yesterday. Did he look all right? I mean, there hasn't been much about him in the papers since he hurt his knee last year. Rumour has it he's finished with football.'

Kate frowned. Finished...

A small doubt wriggled its way into her mind.

Did that put a different complexion on things? She'd read of famous sports people who'd lived the high life while they were on top, only to be stony-broke within months of their retirement.

'He...he looked well enough,' she said carefully, all the while thinking of the state of his clothes, and of his unkempt appearance.

'I'll bet he did.' Estelle grinned. 'Come on, Kate, admit it. He's a hunk, isn't he? Even *you* must concede that.'

Kate bristled. 'What do you mean? Even *me*?'

'Oh, you know. You're not into men, are you?'

'I am so, too,' Kate defended with uncharacteristic fierceness. 'What exactly are you implying?'

Estelle looked both confused and embarrassed. 'Well, I thought...I mean, some of the men here...I mean...I'm not sure what I mean,' she wailed. 'I wasn't sure myself, but when everyone around you keeps saying things then you begin to believe them. I'm sorry, Kate. I really am. It's not me who says things. It's the other secretaries and...and——'

'Their bosses, no doubt!' Kate finished sharply. 'Well, you can tell them from me that they're way off beam.

Just because I've chosen not to marry so far doesn't mean I don't like men. I most assuredly do! So you can all put that in your pipes and smoke it!'

'Kate! Please, don't be so upset. I'm sorry, I really am. Oh, dear, this is awful. I think you're a terrific person and a terrific boss and I...I...'

She promptly burst into tears, forcing Kate to forget her own indignant fury to play the role of comforter. By the time she had the teary-eyed girl settled back at her desk, her own anger had dissipated somewhat. Could she blame people for thinking she was gay? She didn't talk about men, wasn't ever seen with one. As for her clothes...

She glanced down at her savagely tailored navy suit and plain cream blouse. Why did she always dress like that? Was she subconsciously trying to put men off all the time?

Of course she was. No question of it. Men usually frightened the hell out of her. In a personal sense, that was.

Why, was a complex question and one which she had long ceased to analyse. It had seemed self-defeating to worry about the one area of her life where she was a failure. Better to concentrate on what she did do well.

Kate was very proud of her academic achievements, of her highly paid career, of her ability to look after herself without having to lean on anyone. Her very real confidence and efficiency in the workplace probably made her all the more determined to hide her lack of confidence elsewhere, hence her mannish appearance and apparent lack of interest in men. No one could accuse her of being a flop with the opposite sex if she didn't give a hoot about them.

How many people used the excuse of indifference to disguise inner doubts and fears? A lot, she suspected. Especially females, who were plagued these days with the burden of having to look good to be socially acceptable and sexually desirable. God help them if they were plain or overweight or had some other physical disfigurement. For if they did, they were ostracised. Not just when they became adults, but right from the start, first as children, then at a time when acceptance was at its most important. In high school.

Kate shuddered to think of what she had endured at the hands of her classmates because of her problems with her eyes and teeth. The boys had been particularly cruel, teasing her mercilessly, calling her 'four eyes' and 'bucky beaver'. They had especially liked stealing her glasses, without which she was practically blind, enjoying her humiliation at not being able to see properly, only giving her the glasses back after they'd reduced her to tears.

It wasn't long before Kate had been the most introverted girl in her class, her only solace the excellent results she achieved in her exams. Never for her the pleasure of being popular or having a boyfriend. She couldn't even get anyone to partner her at either of her graduations. When she'd asked one boy to partner her on the first occasion, he'd laughed in her face. Needless to say, she hadn't asked anyone else. In the end, she'd made some excuse and hadn't gone to either grad. Not that anyone cared.

Her self-esteem as a female had been totally shot by the time she'd left high school, so when no boys had taken any notice of her at university, Kate had accepted that as perfectly normal. She had withdrawn even further into herself, burying any hurt with more and more study. No wonder she'd always gained distinctions. Underneath, however, she had been just like any other young woman, craving male attention, wanting some boy to take notice of her.

So, by the time she'd reached her last year at university, twenty-two years old and still undated, she was the perfect victim for the likes of Trevor. God, she should have known someone like him wouldn't have been attracted to someone like herself. He was not only handsome but very outgoing and popular.

But Kate had been hopelessly besotted from the first moment he'd taken her for a coffee after lectures one day, then stunned her by asking her out on a date for the following weekend. She'd been on cloud nine for two whole days, till she'd sat herself down on a secluded seat and overheard Trevor talking to his friends on the other side of the low wall behind her.

'If you want an easy lay,' he was boasting, 'then take out one of the ugly ones. Ugly birds are always dying for it! I've got my eye on Kate Reynolds for this weekend. You know, the one with the teeth and the glasses. Let me tell you, lads, I'll have that bird flat on her back before she can say Jack Robinson.'

Kate cringed at how those ghastly, contemptuous words had made her feel—totally crushed, the little that was left of her confidence as a female just ash on the ground. Somehow, she'd been able to get out of that date with some dignity, but the experience had made her crawl even further into her shell.

When she was finally out in the workforce, earning her own money, Kate had fixed the two physical problems that had been the bane of her life—her eyes and her teeth. But by then she was twenty-five, and had never been on a real date with a man. When one eventually asked her, she had refused out of fear. Fear of making a fool of herself, fear of his finding out she was still a virgin, fear of sex itself.

Her virginity had become a neon-light hurdle in her mind when it came to having a relationship with a man. And as each year went by it got worse. Gradually, she'd found herself eliminating all of those little signals a woman sent out to a man in the game of sex, so that she wouldn't have the problem of rejecting any advances, wouldn't have to make *any* decisions where men were concerned.

She'd stopped wearing make-up and perfume. She always wore her hair up. She never wore jewellery. Her clothes had become almost asexual in both line and colour—black, grey or navy suits, teamed with either cream or white blouses. There were no reds, no electric-blues, no emerald-greens. Not even a hint of pink.

The upshot of it was that finally no man gave her a second look and she was able to take the safer, less risky course in life as a single career woman. She lived for her work, filling in what leisure hours she had by going to the theatre, reading and playing bridge.

And she had been content, in a way, till yesterday. Yesterday had shown her that underneath her spinsterish ways lay a woman who could respond to a man as much as the next woman. Suddenly, her life seemed pathetically empty. And hideously lonely. If she kept on like this, what would happen to her in twenty years' time? What would she have?

Nothing.

And no one.

She had to take a stand now, had to start facing her fear of men and sex. *Had* to, before it *was* too late.

Reaching out her hand, she slipped open the drawer and extracted the note that had come with the roses.

This was where she could start, accepting this dinner invitation from Roy. It didn't matter if it was only in appreciation. It didn't matter if she never saw him again. It was a start.

Kate dragged in a deep breath, letting it out in a shuddering sigh. The decision had been made. She would ring Roy and say yes.

But actually picking up that telephone and making such a call was not so easy. Kate kept putting it off, telling herself she would do it after the meeting she had later that morning, then after she'd finished her monthly report on the overseas stockmarkets, then after she'd checked out what the dollar was doing against the yen that day.

Her list of postponements grew, till in the end self-disgust impelled her to snatch up the receiver and dial that number. When it started ringing, sick butterflies crowded in her stomach, but she refused to hang up.

Roy answered on the sixth ring, merely reciting his number. His voice sounded a little fuzzy, as though he'd been asleep.

'Roy? It's Kate . . . Kate Reynolds.'

'Kate!' The pleasurable surprise in his voice startled her. 'You got the roses?'

'Yes . . . yes, I did, and they're just beautiful. Thank you so much.'

'My pleasure. And it's me who's grateful. I've had time to think about what happened and I'm still astonished at what you did, leaping into the fray like that without any concern for your own safety.'

Kate's laughter eased her excruciating tension. 'I didn't really stop to think. If I had I might have stayed in my office.'

'Not you. You're one heck of a brave lady.'

Blushing, Kate gripped the receiver with both hands to stop them from shaking. 'Roy...'

'Yes?'

'About dinner...'

'Yes?'

'I...I'd like to accept.'

'You *would*?'

Now he sounded a little shocked. Hadn't he really meant the offer?

Of course he hadn't, she realised bleakly. Yet with an underlying, gut-wrenching relief. She'd tried, hadn't she? It wasn't her fault she'd failed.

'That's great!' he stunned her with. 'What about tonight?'

'Tonight?' she repeated blankly, her head whirling.

'Yes, if you're free. I could pick you up at your office. There's a tavern down near the quay which serves a fantastic buffet. What do you say? That suit you?'

'I...well, yes, I guess so.'

'You don't sound so sure. If you'd rather go home and change, then say so. It's just that I live in the city and you know what the traffic's like. Not only that, I'm between cars at the moment.'

Between cars and between jobs, she realised, her mind slowly getting back into gear.

'My poor old chariot died a couple of days ago,' he continued blithely, 'and I haven't had the time or the energy to get a new one.'

Didn't have the time? Yet he was home at three in the afternoon. Didn't have the money, more like it. Kate began to feel guilty about forcing the dinner issue. Still, a buffet meal shouldn't set him back too much, and she would make sure she didn't order any expensive drinks.

It was with some shock after her return to cool, considerate reasoning that Kate noticed her hands were still shaking. It's because I've done it, she accepted with an odd mixture of satisfaction and panic. I've accepted a date with a man. Not any man, either. A gorgeous, young, sexy man.

'What time should I pick you up?' he was asking.

'Oh—er—how about seven?'

'You work back till seven every night?'

'Pretty well.'

'Then it's high time you didn't. Fact is, it's high time you stopped doing a lot of things, Kate Reynolds, and started doing others. I'll be there at six. Be ready.'

He hung up, leaving her staring in utter bewilderment into the receiver till the penny dropped.

Kate groaned her dismay as she too hung up.

'I forgot to tell him I'm not gay,' she moaned aloud. 'Oh, lord!'

Squeezing her eyes shut, she slumped back in her chair. But as she hugged her embarrassment to herself in silent misery, Roy's assertions began filtering back into her mind. She knew pretty well what she was supposed to stop doing. But what was it she was supposed to start? Going out with men? Or going to bed with them?

She snapped forward on the chair, green eyes flying open. Dear heaven, what had she just got herself into?

CHAPTER THREE

KATE looked at her watch. It was nearly four. In just over two hours Roy would be here.

For a few seconds, her whole mind seemed to go to mush. She couldn't think. A shudder ran through her. Fortunately, at that moment Estelle came in with some letters for her to sign, forcing Kate to regather her wits.

'Would it be all right if I left a few minutes early this afternoon?' the girl asked while Kate put pen to paper. 'I'm going to a concert at the Entertainment Centre tonight and it takes ages for me to get home to Minto and back in again. I'll put these letters in the post on my way to the station and work through my lunch-break tomorrow to make up for it.'

Kate appreciated Estelle's problem with the distances she had to travel, and often let her leave early. But today she had an ulterior motive in happily letting Estelle leave so early. The last thing she wanted was for her secretary to be around when Roy arrived. Not that Estelle ever stayed till six.

'Yes, of course,' Kate agreed readily.

'You really are a terrific boss,' the girl returned, then hesitated. 'I'm awfully sorry over what happened earlier, Kate. If anyone ever says anything to me about you in future I'm going to give them short shrift, believe me!'

31

Kate tried not to colour but failed. Estelle gave her another apologetic glance, picked up the letters, and retreated tactfully without saying another word.

The incident reminded Kate, however, of her earlier resolve to start changing her life. She'd been proud of herself for making that call and saying yes to Roy. Yet he'd only had to make a simple sexual innuendo and she'd started quaking with fear. Truly, this would not do, not do at all! She had to get her act together and do some real changing.

First things first, she decided. Her appearance!

Jumping to her feet, she hurried into the bathroom and examined her reflection in the mirror, trying to look at herself without bias, without letting the memories of herself as a teenager influence her assessment.

Was she ugly?

No...

Plain?

Not altogether, came the honest answer.

Her features were quite even, her eyes a nice green colour, her mouth quite presentable now that her teeth were straight; her hair, though irritatingly frizzy, was a rich, vibrant red. Her complexion was a definite minus, however, being pale, easily sunburnt and inclined to freckle. Never for her a warm golden tan or the look of the healthy outdoors. Her lips were rather colourless as well.

All in all she had a washed-out look around her face, emphasised perhaps by the bright Titian of her hair. She didn't do herself any favours by not wearing make-up, that was for sure. A bit of jewellery wouldn't go astray either, especially since she always wore her hair up.

Inspiration struck and with rapidly moving fingers she pulled the pins out of her hair and raked it through. She shook her head and the thick mass of tight curls fluffed out all over her shoulders and halfway down her back.

Kate sighed. She wished she had the guts to wear it like that. It looked . . . wild. But it was too much of a change after years of wearing it up. She wouldn't feel right, or comfortable.

No, she thought as she swiftly compressed it again into her usual knot, stabbing the pins back in. Free-flowing hair was for free-flowing spirits. She was a long way off being that.

But she conceded she could do something when it came to her face. A little foundation, blusher, eye-shadow, mascara, lipstick. In fact, she would dash out and buy some as soon as Estelle left. Then she would set about doing something to make her navy blue suit look a little less starchy. Perhaps she would remove the blouse and add a scarf . . .

'Wow!' was Roy's first comment when he saw her.

For a split second, Kate was too consumed with her own feelings on seeing *him* to worry about his re-action to her own improved appearance. For dear heaven, he was even more devastatingly attractive with that stubble shaved off.

His face still wasn't classically handsome, but it was very strong and male. And those eyes! Deep and blue as the ocean on a clear summer's day, they drew Kate into their depths till she was floundering for breath. Yet to look down was to see that incredible body of his displayed to perfection in a fitted pair of black trousers and a stylish, multi-patterned shirt in black and white. His thick black wavy hair completed a breathtaking package of raw sex appeal.

'Is this the same Ms Kate Reynolds I met yesterday?' he was saying with a lilt in his voice and a twinkle in his eye. 'Or has some other creature taken possession of her body?'

The teasing compliment brought a flush to Kate's cheeks. Her smile was shaky, but she was able to say thank you without feeling that Roy was flattering her unduly. In all honesty, she'd been quite thrilled herself with the transformation she'd been able to achieve since Estelle's departure.

The lady in the cosmetics department of the nearby store had been so helpful, actually applying the make-up for her, since Kate had little idea. And what a difference it had made. Why, she looked positively glowing by the time the salesgirl had finished.

Then, as she'd gone to leave the shop, her eye had been taken by the costume jewellery section. One pair of earrings particularly appealed. They were quite large gold drops which seemed to suit her long neck, as well as pick up the gold on the buttons on her navy suit. Once she discarded her severe white blouse, displaying a bare-skinned V between the lapels, her transformation was complete. She was sure she couldn't have felt more surprised—or more excited— than Cinderella going to the ball.

Seeing the genuine admiration in Roy's eyes was like the icing on the cake. She *was* attractive, his appreciative gaze told her. She *was* desirable. She was . . . not gay, Kate remembered suddenly.

Her stomach somersaulted. Really, she had to set him straight about her sexuality. And quickly. To not do so would be stupid and potentially embarrassing.

But correcting his quite understandable mistake was almost as embarrassing.

'Roy...' she began nervously.

'Yes, Kate?'

They were both still standing in her office, Roy near the open doorway, Kate at the side of her desk.

'I—er—there's something I have to tell you.'

His smile was wry. 'Don't I already know?'

'No. You don't.'

He frowned and folded his arms. 'I'm all ears.'

'And I'm not gay,' she blurted out.

He blinked, his arms unfolding as a slow smile spread across his face. 'So! My male instincts didn't let me down. I found it hard to believe it when you said you were. I even lost sleep over it.' His smile became a grin. 'Kate Reynolds, you naughty lady, do you lie like that all the time, just to put a poor guy off?'

Kate didn't make any conscious decision to be totally frank. The words just came tumbling out.

'I didn't really lie, Roy. I *don't* go out with men. I'm a spinster. I live by myself and I like it that way. At least, I did...till today.'

He looked so startled that she felt she had to explain further or leave him thinking she had designs on him. Much as she was very pleased with her improved appearance, and much as she found Roy extremely attractive, she wasn't stupid enough to think a celebrity like him would ever want more from her than this one dinner date. Whatever Roy's motives were for taking her out tonight, they were not because he'd been smitten yesterday. They were probably a mixture of gratitude and boredom. Maybe he was not only between cars and between jobs, but between women.

'Don't look so worried,' she said, her soft laughter mocking herself more than him. 'I'm not about to ask you to move in with me. The truth is, I enjoyed your company yesterday, Roy, and it set me thinking that I might have been silly, not giving men a chance in my life. So perhaps it's me who should be grateful to you, Roy, not the other way round.'

He simply stared at her, totally lost for words.

Kate smiled, pleased with her speech, pleased with the way she was taking control, not only of her life, but of tonight. There she'd been, getting herself all worked up over nothing. Roy was not some bogey-man to be afraid of, even if he did have far too much charm and sex appeal for his own good.

'Shall we go?' she suggested, picking up her black clutch bag and walking forward. Her briefcase, she decided, would have to stay at the office overnight. So would her blouse and the cosmetics she had purchased.

The corner of Roy's mouth lifted as she came towards him, a low chuckle escaping from the lop-sided smile. 'I knew you'd be a woman of surprises, Kate Reynolds. I just didn't know how many.' And, linking an arm through hers, he escorted her through the outer office and to the bank of lifts where a couple of Kate's colleagues were waiting.

One of them was a secretary who Kate was sure would have contributed to the rumours about her sexuality. She was an infernal gossip and a busybody. The girl did a double take when she saw the way Kate looked, then almost fainted when she saw who she was with. Even if she didn't recognise Roy as a famous footballer, she certainly was seeing a young, sexy, gorgeous man holding Kate close to his side and looking for all the world like a genuine date.

'By the way,' Kate whispered to Roy as they too waited for the lift to arrive, 'I know who you are. My secretary told me. Sorry I didn't recognise you.'

'I'm not,' he whispered back. 'It was a very pleasant change from being besieged by teeny-boppers and footie groupies. By the way, why is that girl staring at you like that?'

'Oh, *her*. She thinks I'm gay as well.'

'Does she, now? Shall we shatter her illusions?'

Before Kate could protest, Roy kissed her on the ear, then on her cheek, then, tipping her chin towards him, covered her mouth ever so slowly with his.

She froze, holding her breath till his head lifted, telling herself to smile, not to look as if someone had just punched her in the stomach.

'She's looking as if she doesn't believe what she's seeing,' he murmured into her startled lips. 'I think she needs another dose of shattering.'

This time his kiss was not at all light, and it was Kate who was shattered.

'I think she's finally convinced,' Roy said after his tongue and lips had retreated.

Kate's own tongue and lips had, by this time, gone into cardiac arrest, so that when she tried to speak she couldn't. Thankfully, the doors of the lift slid open at that moment and Roy ushered her forward into the mêlée of people still departing the building. He didn't seem to mind the crush, turning her round and pulling her back hard against him.

When the lift stopped at the next floor down and more people got in, Roy pulled her back even closer

till she could feel every inch of the front of his body.
Heat claimed the entire surface of her skin. Her head
began to whirl.

And then they were on the ground floor and surging
forward into cooler air. Not a moment too soon either.
For Kate was on the verge of real panic, unable to
cope with the alien feelings racing through her body.
One part of her had wanted to sink back into him,
to surrender her will to his in a kind of blindly submissive rush. The rest had twisted tight into a savage
knot within her, ready to unravel at any second. She
could see herself running screaming from the building,
uncaring where she went as long as it was far away
from this man—this *boy*—who could turn her into a
vulnerable mess in so short a period of time.

'What's wrong, Kate?' Roy asked, his hand on her
arm halting her imminent flight.

She turned wide green eyes up to him, her breathing
heavy.

'Did I embarrass you back there? If I did, I'm
sorry.'

'No,' she croaked out. 'You didn't embarrass me.'
What you did was *terrify* me. Who would believe I
could feel like that? she thought agitatedly. So quickly,
so overwhelmingly. OK, so she had never been kissed
before, but were a man's kisses supposed to reduce a
woman to a dazed, desire-filled dope? She doubted
it.

Perhaps, though, she had always been capable of
such sexual susceptibility. Maybe that was why she
had shunned men for so long—because, underneath,
she recognised she was a ready-made victim to their
carnal desires.

Some of the ugly words she'd overheard Trevor say at university popped back into her mind...

'If you want an easy lay, then take out one of the ugly ones. Ugly birds are always dying for it! I'll have that bird flat on her back before she can say Jack Robinson...'

Kate cringed at the memory. What would have happened, she agonised, if she had not overheard Trevor that day, if she had gone out with him the following weekend? Would his boasting have been proven correct? Was her self-esteem so low back then that she might have done anything to savour the illusion of love? She'd always thought she'd turned down Trevor's invitation out of pride. Maybe it had been out of fear, fear that he'd been *right*!

Kate shuddered, and suddenly she was that same destroyed, insecure girl again, full of doubts and fears.

'I...I want to go home,' she said, her voice small, the words haunted, her eyes dropping to the marble foyer floor.

'What?' Roy's tone was short. Annoyed. 'No way, lady. You said you were coming out to dinner with me and that's what you're doing. No more running away for you, Kate Reynolds!'

'Running away?' she repeated dazedly, her eyes lifting.

'Don't go pretending you don't know what I mean. One doesn't have to be Einstein to get the picture. You probably had some rotten experience with some drip of a bloke way back in the dim Dark Ages and have been giving men the cold shoulder ever since. But that was not a cold shoulder you gave me in the lift just now, lady. Nor a cold anything else! So stop this nonsense and let's go!'

Kate stared into those suddenly hard blue eyes, realising at once that there was a tough, uncompromising side to Roy Fitzsimmons which he hadn't shown to her before. Not an unlikely character trait, given his profession. *Ex*-profession, she amended.

But his tough stance was exactly what she needed at that moment. She'd been waffling again. Yes, running scared, as he'd so rightly pointed out. Yet she'd vowed earlier not to do that any more, to face whatever hurdles the opposite sex might present to her. And if she found out she had been hiding an unexpectedly passionate nature, then was that so bad? She could control it, couldn't she?

Of course! She was thirty years old, not a silly young girl. Not a push-over. Certainly not the easy lay Trevor had so nastily prophesied she would be.

But when Roy took her arm again and led her quite forcefully towards the exit, his masterful touch sent a wave of feminine weakness flooding through her, and she found herself wondering just what it would be like to go to bed with this handsome young man. For the first time in her life, Kate began thinking about sex with curiosity, not fear, with an emotion similar to anticipation, not apprehension.

She recognised this was a milestone in her life, a turning-point from which there was no going back. And she owed it all to Roy Fitzsimmons.

CHAPTER FOUR

'HERE we are,' Roy announced after five minutes of brisk walking down the busy city street, steering Kate abruptly from the pavement through an archway and down a flight of narrow stairs, emerging at the bottom into a dimly lit room.

As Kate's eyes adjusted to the light, there materialised every person's fantasy of an old English inn, from the heavy wooden décor to the warm, cheery atmosphere, to the voluptuous wench-waitresses who sidled provocatively between the tables. It was just the sort of place she would imagine Roy frequenting. Raw, ribald and raunchy.

She loved it on sight.

'I think you need a drink first,' he decided, depositing her on a high leather stool at the pub-styled bar before hoisting himself up on to the one next to her. 'What's your poison? No, don't tell me, let me guess. Moselle?'

'That would be nice,' she agreed, doing her best to retain her poise while trying to haul her straight skirt down over exposed knees and thighs.

'Lolly water,' Roy scorned. 'You need a real drink. Merv,' he directed the barman, 'make my lady-friend here a cocktail that will shake the cobwebs from her soul. And give me a beer.'

'Coming right up,' Merv said.

Kate shook her head in amused disbelief at the situation. She tried to imagine what Estelle would think if she saw her boss sitting at a bar with Roy Fitzsimmons. Not that Kate cared what anyone thought. She was having real fun for the first time in years!

The arrival of the cocktail brought a gasp to her lips. For not only was the drink *blue*, but as the barman placed it in front of her he put a match to it and the surface licked with bluish flames. When she gingerly went to pick it up, Roy stopped her.

'You're not supposed to drink it while it's alight, silly,' he laughed. 'Wait. Right, now you can.'

Kate's first sip was tentative. The drink was different from anything she'd ever had before. And it packed a punch she could not hide.

She swallowed, coughed, then laughed. 'Good grief, what's in this thing?' she asked the barman.

'A pretty powerful concoction. It's called a Flaming Lamborghini,' he told her, throwing a mischievous grin over his shoulder as he walked away to serve another customer.

'Now there's a car for you,' Roy remarked. 'How do you think I'd look in a Lamborghini, Kate?'

'I would think you'd have better things to do with your money than buy a car like that,' she advised seriously, only then remembering her decision not to order expensive drinks. 'It's sheer indulgence and not at all economical. The insurance alone would be horrendous.'

'Spoken like a true financial expert. But do I detect a little bit of knowledge about my present circumstances? You wouldn't have been asking questions about my defunct footballing career, would you, Kate?'

'I don't have to ask any questions about you, Roy. My secretary's only too happy to tell me everything. Apparently she's a great fan of yours. Your picture has graced the wall of her bedroom for the last two years. The one where you were hunk of the month.'

Roy groaned. 'Will I never live down that rotten, damned calendar?'

'If it embarrassed you, why do it?'

He grinned. 'The money?'

Kate shook her head. 'Money isn't everything.'

'Try not having any and saying that.'

She looked at Roy's suddenly bleak face and felt sympathy for him squeeze at her heart. 'Sounds as if you were pretty poor once.'

'Dirt-poor. My mum died when I was little and my dad had a lot of health problems. When you live on an invalid pension there's not much left over for extras. We didn't even have an old banger to get around in, so if I want a Lamborghini and can afford one, then I'll have one, and to hell with economy. I've paid in blood, sweat and tears for every cent I've ever earned, and no one will ever tell me how to live my life or how to spend my money.'

Kate stared at him, stunned by his sudden vehemence.

'Sorry,' he apologised on seeing her shock. 'I always over-react when it comes to money. Don't take any notice. Want another drink?'

'I don't think I'd better,' she said, both in deference to his wallet and her own well-being. She wasn't used to spirits and could feel the effect of that drink right down to her toes.

His smile was rueful. 'I don't blame you. Merv's cocktails could fuel rockets to the moon. Shall we proceed to the food, then?'

The smorgasbord was set up on a long wooden trestle-table against a far wall, the spread looking as delicious as Roy had promised. Clearly it was very popular, for there was already quite a queue by the time they made their way over. But the line moved along fairly quickly and it was soon their turn to serve themselves. Kate tucked her bag under her arm, picked up an empty plate from the pile, and tried to make a choice.

'Having trouble?' Roy said after she'd dithered over the various dishes for over a minute.

'I don't know whether to have hot or cold.'

'Have both,' he suggested. 'I am.'

One glance at Roy's plate revealed he was not just having both. He was having *everything*!

She shook her head in disbelief. 'Are you sure you'll be able to eat all that?'

'No trouble. I'm a growing boy.'

The word 'boy' sent a stab of dismay into Kate's heart. For it underlined the transitory nature of the happiness she was finding in Roy's company. She was fooling herself if she thought this one simple dinner date would lead to any more. She was way too old for him. Not to mention not good-looking enough. Why, his usual date was probably around twenty, with a smashing figure, long blonde hair, and sex appeal oozing from limpid blue eyes.

He was just filling in time with her tonight for some reason. As she'd reasoned earlier, he was probably between women. He would forget about her in a couple of days, whereas she would be left with a disturbingly changed attitude to life. Going home to that empty flat every night would never hold the same peace and contentment as it once had.

Kate suspected her spinster days were over. But would she ever recapture this carefree joy with another man? Was there some other male somewhere whose kisses would make the earth move under her feet, whose touch would send electric shivers charging through her veins?

She hoped so. But somehow...she doubted it.

'What's wrong?' Roy said, displaying that uncanny knack he had of tapping into her mood changes.

With a sheer effort of will she shrugged off the sudden bleakness of spirit to smile at him. Treasure these moments, her heart whispered to her. Treasure this night. For there might never be another...

'Someone must have walked over my grave,' she said by way of excuse.

'You're probably just hungry. Come on, give me that plate. You hold mine while I choose for you.'

She laughed delightedly while he piled the plate up with an assortment of foods that rivalled his own for their total lack of combination. Salads sat beside curry, which overlapped sweet and sour pork, which crept on to an assortment of cold meats. Finally two bread rolls were dumped on top.

'Done!' he grinned, and grabbed two more bread rolls for himself. 'Now let's put these on a tray, get some cutlery, then go find us an empty table.'

A couple of apparent acquaintances said hello to Roy as they made their way back across the crowded room. He greeted them with good cheer but kept going. Both men, however, gave Kate a startled look, confirming her opinion of the sort of girl Roy was usually seen with. Once again, her heart sank, but she tried not to show it, keeping a bright smile on her face.

'Here we are,' Roy said, balancing the tray on the table of an empty wall booth. 'Plenty of room and absolute privacy. Sit down, Kate. I'll attend to this.' And with efficient movements, he set the table within seconds, handing the empty tray over to a passing waitress and ordering a bottle of white wine that sounded very expensive.

'I don't mind drinking the house wine,' Kate lied.

Roy grimaced and sat down. 'Well, I do.'

'But bottled wine is awfully expensive in these places.' She frowned.

'Are you worrying about money again?'

'Well, I——'

'Don't!' he cut in firmly. 'This is my shout and I have no intention of counting pennies.'

'Do you *ever* count pennies?' she asked with a wry smile.

His returning smile was just as wry. 'Not if I can help it.'

'What if they run out?'

'Then I'll go out and earn some more.'

'How?'

Now he grinned. 'Is this your sneaky way of finding out what I do for a crust these days?'

She shrugged and picked up her fork. 'Not really. I'm just curious about you, that's all.'

'What if I don't want to tell you?'

She blinked her surprise. 'Why wouldn't you want to tell me? Is it something you're ashamed of?'

'Good God, no,' he laughed. 'I'm not ashamed of anything I've ever done.'

'What about that calendar?'

'Yeah, well, that was different. I didn't realise I would have to take off *all* my clothes.'

'*All*?' Kate made a mental note to ask Estelle to bring that picture to work.

'There was a strategically placed towel,' he went on drily, 'but it was pretty obvious I was starkers. The guys in my league team gave me heaps about it for ages. Dad wasn't too impressed either.' Roy chuckled in fond memory. 'He said he couldn't hold his head up down at the local. Made me promise never to do a thing like that again while he was alive.'

'You and your dad are very close, aren't you?'

'We *were*,' Roy said.

Kate stared at him, frowning her confusion.

'Dad died last year,' he elaborated curtly. 'Cancer.'

'Oh, Roy... Oh, I'm so sorry. I didn't realise.'

'That's all right. You couldn't have known. It's all for the best anyway. He'd suffered enough. And at least I don't have to worry about embarrassing him with anything I ever do these days.'

Kate detected an odd note in Roy's last words, as though he *was*, in fact, doing something these days his dad might find embarrassing. He'd certainly side-stepped telling her what his present job was, yet he had to have some occupation or he wouldn't even be able to afford this meal, let alone those flowers yesterday. Long-stemmed red roses were not cheap.

'But enough about me,' Roy resumed, putting the subject of his father firmly aside. 'I want to know more about you, Miss Kate Reynolds, of Foreign Investments. Have you been at ICAF a long time?'

'Three years.'

'And before that?'

'I was a dealer at a merchant bank.'

'Wow, that's a high-pressure job. No wonder you got out. And what degree did you do to make you into such a financial whiz-kid?'

'I did the bachelor of financial administration course at the Armidale University.'

'How many years is that?'

'Three. Four if you want to do honours.'

'Which you did, of course.'

'Why "of course"?' she asked somewhat archly.

'No need to take offence, Kate, but it's obvious you're one smart cookie.'

'Being smart is not always a recipe for happiness,' she muttered into a spoonful of sweet and sour.

'Neither is being able to play football. I was halfway to being a lawyer when my sporting career took off. Or should I say took over...'

Kate's eyes snapped up, her mouth gaping a little. 'A lawyer?'

Roy rewarded her shock with a sardonic smile. 'Don't I look intelligent enough?'

'Well, yes, of course, but I...I mean...it's just that you...you...'

'It's just that footballers are supposed to be thick,' he finished drily. 'Is that what you were trying to say?'

'Not at all. I would hate to think I'd stereotype people on their looks, or their work. It's just that law is so staid and serious a profession and I simply don't see you fitting that mould. You're too much *fun* to be a *lawyer*!'

Roy almost choked on one of his bread rolls. 'And there I was,' he laughed, 'thinking of going back to finish my degree. Now I'm not sure I'll be able to attend lectures with a straight face. But thank you for the compliment. It *was* a compliment, wasn't it? You don't mean you find me superficial and shallow?'

'Are you superficial and shallow?'

'Often. Are you?'

'Never.'

'I can believe that.'

She looked into those beautiful blue eyes of his, hating the teasing lights she found there, wishing he were ten years older and not nearly so gorgeous. But then he wouldn't be who he was, wouldn't delight her soul so much. Or was it her body he was delighting?

'But in a way, that's good,' he went on with mock-seriousness. 'I need someone solid to keep me on the straight and narrow. I've lived the life of Riley too long.'

'You mean you want me to be a kind of watch-dog?'

'Would you like that role, Kate?'

I'd like any role you want to give me, came the unnerving realisation.

'I doubt I'd ever be in a position to do the job properly,' she said with admirable nonchalance. 'Sounds like the job for a wife.'

'So it does,' he drawled, his eyes locking on to hers. 'So it does...'

There was an interminable period of time when he just kept looking at her with an irritatingly unreadable expression on his face. Then suddenly he seemed to shake himself both mentally and physically, before returning his attention to his meal.

'What do you think of the food?' he said. 'Good, isn't it?'

'Very,' she agreed, and slowly let out her own long-held breath. Really, no man should have such eyes, she decided almost angrily. They were far too perturbing, in both their beauty and their probing quality. She felt they laid bare her soul for him to see while she gained not a single glimpse of his. He was almost as much of a mystery as the first moment she'd spotted him lying on that park bench. She still didn't even know what he did for a living these days.

The wine arrived, somewhat belatedly, but Roy didn't complain. He simply poured out two glasses, then fell to tucking into his food with relish.

Kate did likewise, and soon the food had restored her good spirits.

'What about dessert?' Roy asked after he'd successfully demolished every morsel on his plate.

Kate was still struggling through hers. 'I couldn't!'

'Drink up, then.' He topped up her glass.

'Are you trying to get me drunk?'

'What else?'

'I think you should order black coffee instead of dessert.'

'You can have that back at my place.'

Her heart almost jumped into her mouth, but she raised relatively steady eyes. 'Who said I was coming back to your place?'

'I just did.'

Her sigh was exasperated. 'Did anyone ever tell you that you're bossy and arrogant?'

'No.'

She shook her head. 'I should refuse, just to teach you a lesson in modesty.'

'I've already had that, after the calendar episode.'

Kate laughed. 'You mean you haven't taken your clothes off since?'

'Not in public. I do give private showings, however,' he drawled. 'Are you requesting one?'

Kate flushed fiercely and didn't know where to look. For of course she had already undressed him in her mind a couple of times.

'I've embarrassed you again,' he said softly. 'Sorry, but I couldn't resist. It's been a long time since I've been with a lady capable of blushing.'

Kate's glare was reproachful. 'That's nothing to be proud of.'

'No,' he said slowly. 'No, it isn't. So will you do me the honour of being the first real lady to grace my home, Kate?'

'Only if you promise to behave like a gentleman.'

He pretended to be affronted. 'Kate! How could you think I would ever be anything but a gentleman in your presence?'

'The man who kissed me in front of the lifts was no gentleman,' she reminded him ruefully.

'Ah, but that was only acting, for the benefit of your nasty-minded colleagues. I promise to not only keep my clothes on but my mouth shut.'

She pulled a face at him. 'How can you talk if you keep your mouth shut?'

He clicked his fingers. 'Damn! Didn't think of that. OK, I promise not to try seducing you. How's that?'

'A lie, most probably,' she said before she could snatch it back. But, having said it, she refused to look either flustered or embarrassed.

'Kate! I'm shocked!'

'Like hell you are. I may not have much experience with men, but I can recognise a line when I hear one. I'll come back to your place for coffee, Roy, but I don't want you imagining for one moment I'll let you amuse yourself with me out of boredom. When and if I go to bed with a man it will be because that man means something special to me, and I to him. Do I make myself clear?'

'Perfectly.'

'Well, do you still want to take me home for coffee?'

'I have only one thing to say to that, Kate . . .'

'What?'

'Do you like it white or black? The coffee, that is,' he added with a wicked grin.

CHAPTER FIVE

THE temperature outside had dropped considerably over the hour or so they'd spent inside. Sydney in April usually had balmy days, but the evenings were invariably crisp. A fresh breeze whistled down the city street, making Kate shiver as it raced around her knees and up her skirt.

'Is it a long walk to your place?' she asked Roy. 'Should we catch a taxi? I'll pay if you're short.' The meal and drinks had not cost too much, but she had no idea of Roy's real financial state. For all she knew, he might be almost flat broke.

'Can't you see I'm not short?' he said, holding his arms wide and grinning down at her from his considerable height.

'You know I didn't mean your height,' came her droll reproof. 'Truly, Roy, do you always make a joke of *everything*?'

'Not usually, but you seem to have had a tonic effect on my sense of humour.' And, laughing, he suddenly hugged her, the quite rough action slamming her against his broad chest with such force that all the breath was knocked out of her body. Not content with that, he picked her up and swung her round, almost knocking into a passer-by, who had to skip to one side to avoid Kate's legs.

'Watch it, buster,' the man grumped.

'Sorry,' Roy returned breezily.

The man muttered some other irritable remark before moving on, head down, briefcase clasped tightly in his hands. A breathless Kate stared after him, thinking to herself that that was her most nights, hurrying home after work all by herself, cocooned in her own little world. She herself had passed couples sometimes as they'd laughed and horsed about in the type of semi-rough-house play lovers often indulged in.

Lovers?

Kate pulled herself up short, swallowing as she glanced up at the handsome young man next to her. Now that was the stuff dreams were made of. She and Roy would never be *real* lovers.

'Don't let that grouch upset you,' he said, giving her a quick squeeze where his hand still rested lightly on her waist.

'I...I'm not upset.'

'Funny, you looked it there for a moment.'

'No. Not at all.' She forced a bright smile to her mouth. 'I'm not even cold any more.'

'Well, I am. Let's hurry. My place is only two blocks away. We'll be inside sipping coffee in less than ten minutes. Here! Give me your hand. Let's go.'

Kate was so taken with the simple pleasure of racing along a street holding hands that she didn't think too much about where Roy's place could possibly be. She rather supposed he rented a couple of rooms in some seedy old boarding-house or hotel near the quay area.

It *was* near the quay, but the cement and glass sky-scraper Roy stopped in front of was far from seedy. It was near-new, sparkling and outrageously expensive-looking.

'You rent in *here*?' exclaimed a dumbfounded Kate as Roy propelled her through the revolving glass doors and into the twenty-floor building. Steering her across the marble-floored lobby, he said 'Hi' to the two uniformed security men seated behind the huge semi-circular reception area before striding over to the bank of lifts, where he pressed the up button. Only then did he bestow an amused glance on Kate's astonished face.

'I did tell you I wasn't short of a buck. And I don't rent. I own this place, lock, stock and barrel, invested all my spare cash into it a couple of years back. Besides the security aspect of a sound property investment, I've always got a roof over my head.'

'Some roof! Next thing you'll tell me you're in the penthouse.'

'One of them. There are four, actually.'

'Oh, my God,' she groaned, embarrassed by all her earlier thoughts about his financial status. Or lack of it. 'You're rich.'

'No, not rich. Not *yet*. But I'm working on it.'

The lift doors shot back and they walked in. Roy pressed the penthouse floor button, the doors hissed shut, and they started upwards.

'Are you ever going to tell me what you do for a living these days?'

'Not for a while. I like keeping you in the dark. I like your not having preconceptions about me.'

She shook her head in exasperation. 'Just as well I'm not a curious sort of woman,' she muttered. But she *was*. At least, about him. 'Can't you give me a clue?'

His sideways glance held a mischievous glint. 'No clues. If you're a good girl, I might tell you in a week or so.'

Kate's heart leapt. Did that mean he planned to ask her out again? Now this was one thing she refused to let go of. But just then the lift reached its destination and the doors slid back to reveal a wide circular corridor with a plush blue-green carpet on the floor and seascape paintings on the wall. No doors or windows in evidence, however.

'This way,' Roy said, and directed her round to the left, where shortly they came to a recessed door into which he slid a key.

Any questions Kate had for him about his social intentions regarding herself were forgotten once she was inside his apartment.

Never had she seen such a place!

The foyer was nothing short of opulence incarnate, with a marble floor underfoot, mirrored walls all around, and a huge crystal chandelier high above in the vaulted ceiling. To the right, a black wrought-iron staircase wound its elegantly fashioned way up to a gallery level above, which was hidden from view by a solid wall. Straight ahead, however, an archway opened up into a sumptuously furnished living-room that looked as if it had materialised from the pages of *Home Beautiful*.

'Oh, Roy,' Kate murmured, stepping forward on to deep-piled cream carpet in a kind of daze. 'This is so beautiful...'

'I don't use this room much,' he admitted on joining her. 'That's why it's so tidy.'

Not merely tidy. It was exquisite, decorated tastefully in olive-greens and dull golds, with an arrangement of deep sofas and armchairs in front of a marble fireplace, elegantly draped curtains framing a huge window and a grand piano filling a far corner.

Kate wandered over to it, running a light admiring hand across the polished wooden top of the instrument.

'Do you play?' she asked Roy.

'Not a note. Do you?'

'No, but I'd love to.'

'Why don't you take lessons? Then you could come and practise here. Give me a good excuse to see more of you.'

She turned to look at him, hoping she didn't look the way she felt. Totally confused. For what *was* she doing here? What did Roy really want with her? Mere gratitude did not extend this far.

Much as she'd like to believe he found her an attractive, interesting and desirable woman, those old tapes kept playing in her mind, reminding her that if this was so then he was about the first man who had. Certainly the first incredibly handsome, wonderfully built, super athlete who had!

'Do you need an excuse?' she asked, trying to sound carefree while inside her stomach twisted into knots in anticipation of his answer.

He started to walk across the room towards her, the look in his eyes making her heart thud wildly. He's going to kiss me, she realised. He's going to take me in his arms and kiss me and I don't believe this is happening and I——

The telephone rang, sharp and insistent in the sudden quiet of the room.

'Damn,' he muttered, throwing her an almost anguished look. 'I'd better answer it.'

'Of course,' she said serenely, while inside she wanted to scream out her dismay. For something told her that the moment had gone, and would never come again.

He turned and went through a door, leaving it slightly ajar.

Even from where she was Kate had no trouble hearing Roy's voice, its deep resonance carrying on the apartment's still air.

'Yes, Ned, you did,' he ground out. 'I hope this is important.'

Kate wondered who Ned was.

'You've got to be joking!' Roy went on frustratedly. 'We've bent over backwards to satisfy that woman. What did she expect?'

Kate blinked at both the harshness and content of Roy's words.

'Good God, she didn't, did she?' he burst forth again. 'Hell, but some of those older broads drive a hard bargain. For her to want all that for the same money the previous blokes charged is outlandish. Someone should tell her that you only get what you pay for. We're a class act, Ned. If they want cheap and nasty, then let them go find it. The next time she rings you pass her on to me. I'll tell her straight what's what!'

Kate's mouth had gone dry as she listened to this mind-numbing speech. A ghastly, almost unbelievable suspicion seeped into her mind. Surely Roy couldn't be doing what it sounded as if he was doing. *Could* he?

She blinked her shock and kept listening.

'No trouble, Ned,' Roy was saying. 'I'm getting used to this by now. Yeah, and I'm getting tough. We have to treat this like the serious business it is. We are not a charity organisation for neglected wives and widows. Damn it all, most of these women have more money than they know what to do with! I refuse to feel any guilt over what we charge. If they don't like what we deliver, then they can go elsewhere. The same goes for those hard-boiled career types who want to be fitted in at all odd hours.'

Oh, my God, Kate thought despairingly. He *was*. He really was! No wonder he was loath to tell her what he did for a living.

'Yeah, you're right,' Roy admitted grudgingly. 'At least they're prepared to pay for the privilege. OK, I'll see what I can do to accommodate most of them. Now hang up, Ned, I have a visitor and I've promised her coffee.' His laughter sounded lewd to Kate's newly opened ears. 'I doubt that, Ned. But you never know your luck. Bye.'

When Kate heard the receiver being replaced she scuttled across to the other side of the living-room and into an intimate dining alcove from where it would have been impossible to overhear that phone call. Clutching her bag tightly to try to stop her hands from shaking, she stared blankly through the uncurtained picture window that overlooked Sydney Harbour. Most people would have been dazzled by such a view at night, with the lit bridge on the left and the white sails of the Opera House on the right. But she didn't notice any of it, blinded by her inner emotional upheaval.

Why, oh, why hadn't she trusted her initial and on-going fears about this date, trusted the suspicion that there was more to it than mere gratitude, trusted the knowledge that she would *not* be attractive to a man like Roy, no matter what pathetic changes she made to her appearance? Then she wouldn't be feeling as she was feeling at this moment. Totally devastated.

A bitter taste invaded her mouth when she recalled what she'd first imagined about Roy, that he might be using his not inconsiderable sex appeal to make ends meet. How right she had been! He was nothing but a charlatan and a con man of the worst order, playing on the vulnerabilities of lonely women like herself, suckering them in with his attentions, making fools of them with his false charm. Once they were suitably smitten, no doubt he would start suggesting they pay for the privilege of his company, and whatever other services he provided.

Kate shuddered to think of them.

'*Here* you are!'

Everything inside her tightened at his voice, but her eyes remained remarkably steady as she turned from where she was standing at the window. She stared at him, wanting to hate him for the amoral bastard he was, but somehow, when she looked at that handsome, smiling face, all she wanted to do was cry.

The tears pricking at her eyes were the catalyst that made a coldly indignant anger replace her wretchedness. She'd vowed once before that no man would make her cry again. And that certainly included the likes of Roy Fitzsimmons.

'I'm sorry, Roy,' she said with an icy composure. 'But I can't stay for that coffee after all. Thank you for the dinner. I enjoyed it very much. But I've just remembered I have an early start tomorrow and I really should be getting home.'

His smile faded instantly. But he said nothing for a few moments, watching her closely with that penetrating gaze of his. 'If you must,' he said at last. 'Let me call you a taxi.'

Relief warred with a quite unreasonable anger. What had she expected? That he would try harder to get her to stay, use that infallible charm of his in an effort to persuade her? One would have hoped that her infatuation with him would have died with the realisation of his true character. But it hadn't. If anything, in one way she was more intrigued with him than ever.

Self-disgust sent an acid edge to her voice.

'Thank you,' she bit out. 'I'd appreciate that.'

'Where shall I say the destination is?'

'North Sydney.'

'You live there with your family?'

'No, I live alone.'

'You have no family?'

Cynicism invaded Kate's heart. No doubt it was imperative that he knew as much as possible about his victims. Knowledge was power. But not where she was concerned. He could know all there was to know about her and it would make no difference. Tonight was the death knell for her where men were concerned, for never would she allow one to get past her defences again. Loneliness was far preferable to this pain. Far, far preferable!

'I have plenty of family,' she returned coldly. 'But none of them lives in Sydney. Now, would you mind calling that taxi?'

He gave her one last frowning look before leaving her, returning a couple of minutes later. 'Security will call when it arrives.'

'It would be quicker if I went down and waited.'

His glance was sharp. 'Are you really in that much of a hurry?'

To get away from you? I would think speed is imperative.

'I'm not used to late nights,' she excused, and began moving towards the front door.

He followed her. 'It's not that late.'

'It will be by the time I get home and into bed. I have work tomorrow, remember?'

'Speaking of tomorrow, can I call you?'

'I think it would be better if you didn't,' she replied coolly.

'I don't agree.'

'You'll be wasting your time.'

Now he was frowning darkly at her. 'There's something here I've missed.'

She totally ignored that remark. 'You don't have to accompany me downstairs. You must be tired.'

Without consciously meaning to, she put a sarcastic barb into that last remark, bringing another sharp look from Roy.

'Why do you say that?' he said as he opened the door for her.

'You look tired.'

'And you look beautiful,' he said softly.

It was the worst thing he could have said. She turned on him, eyes blazing with fury. 'Don't you ever, *ever* pay me false compliments, do you hear me? I'm not beautiful. I'm not even pretty. And I have nothing but contempt for men who think they can flatter their way into a woman's heart!'

She didn't look back as she stalked off, literally shaking with emotion. He caught her at the lift doors, a rough hand on her arm spinning her round to face him. He looked both surprisingly distressed and quite perplexed.

'What in hell's going on here?' he demanded to know. 'What have I done? Is it the apartment, is that it? Do you think I'm some sort of playboy millionaire who wanted you for a one-night stand? Let me assure you that's not the case. I——'

Her hard laughter cut him off. 'I'm sure it isn't. One-night stands don't get the loan of a grand piano. You had something longer-lasting in mind, didn't you?'

'And if I did? Was that so wrong? I like you, Kate. I want to see more of you. I want——'

'I know exactly what you want, Roy Fitzsimmons, but this time you struck out. Next time do your homework a little more thoroughly before you send roses. They're expensive, I gather.'

'Look, Kate, I won't deny sex hadn't entered my mind when I asked you out, but that was before I got to know you better.'

'Oh, please, Roy, spare me the fancy lines. Use them on some of your other lady-friends.'

'What other lady-friends? I haven't taken a woman out in donkey's years.'

The lift doors opened then, Kate throwing Roy a look of total exasperation over her shoulder as she swept inside. Maybe he didn't call what he did with all those women '*taking them out*'. Taking them *in* was more like it!

'No!' she cried out when he went to follow her into the lift, waving her hands at him in distress. 'Please, Roy, if you like me at all, just let me go.'

Startled, he stepped back to stand in the doorway, effectively stopping them from closing. Panic invaded

Kate's heart, for she knew if he touched her then, if he took her in his arms and started making love to her, she might not have the strength to fight him. Somehow, the secret knowledge that she could have him if she wanted him—albeit by paying for him— had brought with it the most wicked temptation.

What if she told him she knew what he was? What if she told him she didn't care? What if she told him she would pay anything to keep the fantasy of his friendship going?

'Please,' she almost sobbed, terrified by the way her mind was going.

'All right,' he agreed reluctantly, stepping back out through the doors. 'But just for tonight.'

The door began to shut and Kate heaved a shuddering sigh of relief.

'I *am* going to call you tomorrow, Kate Reynolds,' he shouted through the rapidly diminishing gap. 'You mark my words!'

The taxi was already waiting at the kerb outside when Kate hurried through the glass doors. She was at home and in bed before ten o'clock, but sleep did not claim her till well after midnight. Marking Roy's words was a very distracting and disturbing thing to do.

CHAPTER SIX

'Is IT true?' Estelle wailed when she returned from morning tea with the other secretaries.

Kate looked up from her desk, frowning. She'd been distracted all morning, absolutely terrified that Roy would call her and she would be forced to make the decision once again to tell him to get lost. 'Is what true?'

'That you went out with Roy Fitzsimmons after work yesterday.'

Kate could feel her cheeks immediately going pink. She'd totally forgotten about the witnesses here at work the previous evening.

'It *is* true!' her secretary exclaimed, utter disbelief in her face and voice.

'Yes, it's true,' Kate agreed, seeing little point in denying it. In fact, on second thoughts, she saw no reason why she shouldn't gain *something* out of last night's fiasco, if it was only to let the other girls at work believe she went out with men like Roy all the time.

Having made this decision, it was imperative to stop blushing and start acting the part with a bit more *savoir-faire*. 'Roy dropped by after you left and asked me out to dinner,' she explained casually. 'So I went.'

'But Cheryl said he ... he ...'

Kissed me in front of the lifts, Kate finished with a silent groan at the memory.

For that was where the attraction had flared to a full-blown infatuation, with Roy's lips on hers. From the first contact of his flesh against hers, Kate had been overcome by a dizzying pleasure such as she'd never felt before, and which she had not in any way forgotten.

It was the memory of that pleasure which was worrying her now. What would she not give to feel like that again, to be swept away into that world where reality ceased to exist, even if only for a short space of time?

'Cheryl also said you looked totally different,' Estelle resumed almost accusingly. 'She said you were wearing make-up and . . . and earrings.'

Kate couldn't help laughing. 'For heaven's sake, Estelle, is it a crime to wear make-up and earrings? You're acting as if I've done something wrong. At least now you won't have any trouble convincing the others your boss is not gay,' she finished drily.

'You can say that again. Cheryl said our hunk of the month was all over you like a rash!'

Kate sighed her exasperation with the girl. 'Now that's an exaggeration. All he did was kiss me once or twice. Don't your boyfriends kiss *you* when you go out?'

Estelle's mouth dropped open. 'You mean Roy Fitzsimmons is your *boyfriend* now?'

Kate sighed her frustration. The more she explained, the more complicated things became. 'Look, we're just friends, right?'

'Oh, sure!' Estelle's expression was knowing. 'People always say that when there's something going on and they don't want anyone to know. You can't fool me, Kate. You're having an affair with him, aren't you? I can always tell when a female is sleeping with a guy. They get all hot and bothered when you talk about them.'

'I am *not* hot and bothered!' Kate defended, though she suspected she might look it. The flush in her cheeks had deepened, and the blood was pumping through her heart like a threshing machine. All she wanted was for Estelle to leave her be and stop talking about that infernal man!

'Sure thing,' the girl said drily. 'You look as cool as a cucumber. Heck, Kate, I could fry eggs on your cheeks.'

'Estelle,' Kate said warningly, 'if you wish to remain my secretary, then you will drop this subject right now. I am not having an affair with Roy Fitzsimmons. If you must know, I doubt I'll ever go out with the man again after last night.'

'Ooh . . . Did he get out of line, did he? I've heard he's a bit of a lad with the ladies. Of course it's only to be expected when a——'

A sudden tap on the open office door cut Estelle off mid-sentence. When she saw Kate rising from her chair, mouth agape, green eyes wide, she whirled round, only to find that the hand which had tapped belonged to the very man whom Kate had just claimed she would never see again.

'Sorry to interrupt,' Roy said. 'But there was no one at the desk outside and I heard voices so I—er . . .' His voice trailed away as both women continued to stare at him in a stunned silence, Estelle, no doubt, with a kind of morbid curiosity, Kate still in a state of utter shock. She'd geared herself up for a telephone call, not a personal visit.

This wasn't fair, she agonised as her gaze took in the sheer macho appeal of the man, all six feet five of him, encased in tight blue jeans and a matching denim jacket. He was back to sporting the unshaven look as well, which, along with his rather windswept black waves, produced a rough-diamond air that was so sexy that it was indecent.

Swallowing, she reefed her eyes back upwards till they locked swords with that incisive blue stare.

'If I'm interrupting something important, Kate, I'll wait outside.'

'Oh, no, Mr Fitzsimmons,' Estelle leapt in, flushing prettily as she stared up at him in open admiration. 'Come right in. I was just leaving, wasn't I, Kate?'

She scuttled out, shutting the door behind her, leaving Kate to face the enemy with no weapons at all except what she could muster from the mess within herself. For the sight of him had only served to remind her how utterly, utterly gorgeous he was. Gorgeous and vital and virile and . . . available. It was just a matter of how much money he wanted.

Curling her fists tightly, she leant on the desk for support and eyed him with what she hoped was a suitably stern look. 'I thought I made my feelings quite plain last night, Roy,' she said stiffly.

'Not to me, you didn't,' he countered. 'You left me totally confused.'

'Oh, come, now——'

'No, you come, now, lady,' he ground out, anger flaring a dull red across his cheekbones. 'One minute we were having a good time together. The next . . . whammo! I thought somebody had plunged me into the Antarctic. I want to know what gives.

What happened, exactly, to cause such a dramatic change?'

'I think you know the answer to that, if you put your mind to it.'

'Well, you're wrong there. I've put my damned mind to it all night and I'm no closer to a solution except the one I first thought of. Because you were OK till we went up to the penthouse and then you changed. So it *was* the penthouse, is that what you're saying?'

'No.'

'Then tell me, damn it!'

His anger stunned, then infuriated her, as did his stubborn persistence in coming here personally. Why hadn't he just let it go? So he lost out on a prospective client. So what? There were sure to be other fish in the sea. Schools of them, from the sound of that phone-call last night.

'I told you,' she said coldly. 'I don't go out with men.'

'Is that so?' he flung back. 'Well, might I remind you that you went out with *me* last night, lady, and I happen to be a man.'

'Of sorts, I suppose!'

The insult sent all the breath rushing from his body. He strode across the room, his face darkening further. Kate shrank back against her chair, fearing the simmering violence underlying his angry movements.

But he didn't touch her. He stayed on the other side of the desk, glaring across at her with eyes of cold steel. 'You'd better explain that remark, Kate Reynolds, or by God I'll be tempted to show you exactly how much of a man I am.'

'Oh, really?' she foolishly taunted. 'And how, pray tell, will you do that? Give me a demo of some touchdowns? I'm afraid you'll be wasting your time. I'm not into football.'

His smile was not amused. 'No, I have something more primitive in mind. Like putting you across my knee and smacking that cheeky backside of yours till you regain your manners!'

'You wouldn't dare!'

'You have only one way of stopping me, and that's by telling exactly what's got into that finance-filled head of yours about me. And I want the bare facts. No more double-talk!'

'Are you sure you could stand to hear the truth in the cold light of day?' she jeered.

'Much better than you'll be able to stand your punishment if you don't tell me.'

'Very well,' she sniffed. 'But don't say you weren't warned. I know what you are, Roy Fitzsimmons. I know exactly how you've been earning your living since you gave up footall. I overheard the telephone call you received from that Ned person last night, and one would have to be stupid not to put two and two together.'

She drew herself up tall and straight, indignant pride fuelling a self-righteous anger. 'So you see, once I realised the truth I knew exactly why you asked me out, why you wanted to ask me out again, *and* why you're here today. You thought I was one of those lonely, hard-boiled career women with more money than sense, and whom you could fit in at odd hours. But you made a mistake this time, didn't you? Your prey found out about you before you had your talons well and truly in place! You struck out this time, lover-boy.'

Never had she seen anyone as floored as the man opposite her. He stared at her, obviously shaken. Clearly he'd had no idea that his conversation with that seedy Ned person could be overheard, or that what could be heard would be so telling.

'What really infuriates me,' Kate swept on, 'is that I could have believed, even for a moment, that a man like you would be interested in someone like me. But that's how it works, doesn't it? You pick your victims well, never going for anyone young or pretty. You like them to be terribly flattered by your attentions—bowled over, in fact. That way they can't think straight. Then after you've taken them to bed once, you——'

'Taken them to bed?'

'Oh, for pity's sake, give up the innocent act, Roy. Your cover's blown. I know you're nothing but a gigolo.'

'A gigolo,' he repeated in such a numbed voice that Kate had a momentary pang of doubt.

The doubt grew while he continued to stare. But gradually the startled look in his eyes cleared and he cocked his head on one side, looking at her with a type of interested curiosity. Then suddenly, he laughed. It was a harsh, almost angry sound.

Oddly, it shocked her. Maybe underneath she'd been hoping there was some other explanation for what she'd heard. But it seemed she'd been spot-on. 'So you're admitting it,' she said. 'You *are* leading the life of a gigolo.'

'I'm admitting nothing.'

'But you can't deny that——'

'I'm denying nothing,' he cut in with a strange smile on his face. 'Why should I?'

'I don't find this funny, Roy,' Kate said sharply. 'You hurt me last night.'

'Did I, Kate?' he asked softly. 'How?'

'You . . . you . . .'

'Sent you roses, took you to dinner, gave you a good time. And I paid, remember? Then, when you wanted to go home, I let you. In what way did I hurt you?'

'You . . . you deceived me. I thought you liked me.'

'I *do* like you.'

'You wanted to use me.'

'No, I *wanted* you.'

She gasped as heat flushed the entire surface of her skin. 'Don't say such things.'

'Why?'

'They're lies.'

'*Are* they, Kate?'

'You know they are,' she ground out, livid at his thinking he could con her even now, after she *knew* what he was.

He sighed. 'No, *you* believe they are. And you'll always believe they are, won't you?'

She refused to answer, but her flush was telling.

There ensued a long silence where Kate slumped back down at her desk and Roy continued to stare down at her. The red light that indicated an incoming call came on. Her eyes jerked up to meet Roy's.

'I have to take a call. Why don't you just go?'

'I'm not going anywhwere. Take your call, Kate. I'll wait over here till you're finished.' And, turning, he strode over to the chesterfield, making himself quite comfortable by undoing his denim jacket before sitting down, then cocking one leg over his other knee and splaying both his arms along the back. He looked not only comfortable, but supremely confident.

Kate dragged her eyes away from where his white T-shirt was stretching to accommodate his expanded chest muscles, and snatched up the receiver.

'Kate Reynolds,' she announced with only a shadow of her normal aplomb.

'Kate. It's your mother here.'

Kate felt something tight and defensive curl within her. 'Yes, Mum?'

'Just a reminder call, dear, in case you've forgotten this weekend is the one we put aside for our family reunion.'

'No, I haven't forgotten, Mum. I've taken next Monday off so I don't have to drive back on the Sunday.'

'That's sensible, dear. Now it's just you, isn't it?'

'Yes, Mum, it's just me.'

'No—er—friend . . . you'd like to bring?'

'No.'

The sigh on the other end of the line made Kate's insides tighten further.

'Oh, well, I won't need to make up the guest room, will I?'

'Not this time.'

'Your father and I thought we'd have a barbecue this year.'

'A barbecue's a good idea,' Kate agreed.

'When can I expect you?'

'I'll leave first thing Saturday morning, should be in Armidale around afternoon tea.'

'You will drive carefully, dear, won't you? The roads are awfully busy on the weekends.'

'I'll be very careful.'

'Bye, dear.'

'Bye, Mum.'

Kate hung up, remaining silent and thoughtful for a few seconds.

'Your family lives in Armidale?'

Kate's heart jumped. She'd almost forgotten her visitor, which just showed how much she dreaded the coming weekend. The thought of it had blotted out all her other immediate problems.

'Yes,' she said shortly.

'And you're driving all the way up there by yourself?'

She flashed him a caustic look. 'Amazing what women can do all by themselves these days, isn't it?'

There was no visible reaction to her sarcasm, except perhaps for a slight tightening of his facial muscles. 'I gather you're not looking forward to the visit?'

'You gather correctly. I'm the odd man out, aren't I? No spouse or children to parade for Mummy's and Daddy's approval.'

'Do I detect some bitterness there?'

She shrugged. 'Perhaps. I've ceased to analyse myself.'

'I don't wonder,' he muttered.

She glared at him, but he refused to be cowed, looking back at her with eyes as bold as brass.

'Why don't you take me to Armidale with you?' he suggested. 'I could be your new lover.'

'Don't be ridiculous!'

'Why is it ridiculous?'

'Well, for one thing, my family would not believe I had a lover at all, let alone someone like you. On top of that, I probably couldn't afford you!'

He lifted a sardonic eyebrow, glancing around her executive office. 'Oh, I think you could,' he drawled. 'Admittedly, I'm quite expensive on an hourly rate, but for the whole weekend I could come up with a special deal, just for you.'

Kate hated herself for even listening to him. But there was a certain fascination in what he was saying. Were there really women around who hired men like him for the weekend? 'Thank you for that most generous offer,' she snaked out, 'but no, thanks.'

'Frightened, Kate?' came his soft query.

'Of *you*?'

'No. Of yourself...' He unfolded himself from the chesterfield, making her mouth go dry as he walked slowly towards her.

'What...what are you going to do?' She gripped the armrests of her chair. Her head had started spinning and her heart was thudding madly under suddenly taut breasts. 'If you touch me, I'll scream.'

'I'm not going to touch you, Kate.' He picked up a Biro from her desk and turned a notepad around. 'I'm going to write down your address in North Sydney. What is it?'

'I'm not going to tell you.'

'Yes, you are,' he grated, a steely glint in his eye. 'And you're going to take me to Armidale with you on Saturday.'

'And why would I do that?'

'Because you want to.'

'That's ridiculous!'

'No, it's not. It's perfectly logical. You're weary of going home and having your female ego trampled into the ground. You'd like to have a man on your arm just once. Who better than someone young and

presentable and, yes, high profile? Your family will
never look at you the same way if you turn up with
me, Kate. I promise you.'

It all sounded so wonderful, and so harmless, in a
way. For Roy was quite right. She was very tired of
how her family perceived her. The look on their faces
if she walked in with the fabulous and famous Roy
Fitzsimmons on her arm would almost be worth any
risk.

Yet the risk was just too great. If she hired Roy as
her escort for the weekend, and he turned his charm
upon her full blast, how soon before she was tempted
to hire him a second or a third time? And how soon
before she wanted more than his arm on hers?

That was his plan, of course. To ensnare her into
his clutches, to turn her into one of those women who
would be willing to pay for the pleasure of his
company, whether that company be platonic or sexual.
His quest for the almighty dollar was all-consuming,
it seemed, so much so that he was willing even to
prostitute himself for it.

Despite her sense of outrage Kate could not stop
the question of how much extra he might charge for
that kind of service from slipping into her mind. The
idea of paying him to make love to her had a wickedly
perverse appeal. That would certainly be taking
control of the sexual side of her life, wouldn't it? And
it would certainly take care of any fears she had of
rejection. He would go to great lengths to please her,
to give her her money's worth. She wished just
thinking about such a prospect didn't excite her so
much.

'I won't sleep with you, however,' he stated coolly.
'I never sleep with a client on the first date.'

Kate was stung, both by his arrogant boldness and her own guilty thoughts. 'How very disappointing,' she scoffed. 'As if I would ever sleep with a man who hired himself out by the hour!'

'Oh, I hire myself out by the night as well,' he countered without batting an eyelash. 'When I find a special client—one I personally like—I prefer to stay the whole night. After all, an hour or two hardly does justice to my talents in that department. But I'm sorry, Kate, much as I like you, I must abide by my rules. I insist on finding out more about a woman before I go to bed with her, no matter how much I like her or how much money she offers. Which reminds me, my charges for the weekend will be five hundred dollars a day plus expenses.'

'That's outrageous!'

'Kate, darling, that's cheap. I normally charge twice as much. I'm offering you reduced rates because there won't be any sex involved.'

Kate was flabbergasted, more so when she realised she was actually considering doing this.

'Go on, Kate,' he urged softly. 'Do something wild for once. Hire me.'

She stared at him, knowing that to accept this deal was insanity. It was a trap. She just knew it was a trap!

But she kept thinking about the looks on her family's faces when she arrived with Roy, especially her mother's. What price one's pride and self-esteem? Apparently, one thousand dollars plus expenses.

'All right,' she agreed, then shuddered.

The ruthless satisfaction in those blue eyes should have frightened the life out of her. But a sudden mad recklessness invaded, refusing to let her succumb to the worries and doubts that threatened to invade her conscience. To hell with convention, she thought. To hell with everything. This weekend, she was going to be and have what she wanted, even if it was only pretend.

'One thing, though,' Roy said, interrupting her mental fantasy. 'If you're supposed to be *my* girl-friend for the weekend, then you're going to have to dress a hell of a lot differently to *that*!' And he waved a dismissive hand over her appearance.

She glanced down at her clothes with some dismay. After last night's disaster, she'd reverted to her usual manner of dressing, wearing a severely cut black suit, no make-up and no jewellery.

'You look like a bloody undertaker!'

The accusation revived Kate's sense of self-worth. 'Better than looking like a bimbo!'

'Honey, you couldn't look like a bimbo if you tried. But you could look like the intriguing, very feminine and eminently desirable woman that you are. So bring your credit cards with you, lover. We're going clothes-shopping!'

CHAPTER SEVEN

KATE found it hard to sleep on the Friday night. Was it excitement that kept her awake? Or that cold fear of somehow making a fool of herself when it came to the opposite sex?

One thing that kept going round and round in her mind was amazement at herself for allowing Roy to take total control of the situation the other day. Fancy letting him choose those outrageous clothes for her. And fancy making the outrageous decision to hire him for the weekend in the first place. She had to be crazy!

Yet he'd made it all sound so exciting. And almost imperative!

The man was wicked, there was no doubt about that. Totally and utterly wicked. *And* devious. Why, by the end of their shopping expedition, he'd made her think of him as a friend doing her a favour, when what he was really doing was drawing her deeper and deeper into his sexual trap. The clothes were undoubtedly part of his weaponry in breaking down her defences.

Kate could not deny, however, that she'd looked pretty good in those clothes. They'd made her feel different, too. More confident and outgoing and, yes . . . sexy.

Now that was a new experience for her—feeling sexy. She'd had no idea how deliciously satisfying it was to have a man's eyes rove hotly over her body the way Roy's had when she'd come out in that leather outfit. Not only satisfying, but arousing. Another new experience that—being aroused.

For years, she had buried her sexual feelings, looking away when an erotic part in a movie came on the screen, not reading sexy books, never looking at herself naked in the mirror. Never, *ever* giving in to the temptation to touch herself.

Now, as she lay in bed, one hand drifted lightly down over her satin nightie, and across one of her nipples. It sprang hard against her palm, tingling slightly. Kate shot her hand out from under the sheet, only to see it was shaking. *She* was shaking.

There was no doubt about it, she realised. If and when Roy chose to take advantage of her infatuation with him, she was a goner. Even knowing what he did for a living did not change how she felt in his company. When those gorgeous blue eyes twinkled at her she fairly glowed. When he put his hand, even casually, on her arm she trembled inside.

Groaning, she rolled over and punched her pillow.

'You are a stupid, stupid fool, Kate Reynolds! Why didn't you mind your own business last Monday morning? Why didn't you let those kids pound Roy into little pieces? Then you wouldn't be in this goddamn awful mess!'

Roy rang the front doorbell of her flat right on eight o'clock the next morning. Kate had been up for literally hours, primping and preening as she'd never primped and preened in her life. She alternately loved then hated herself in the tight chocolate-brown ski-pants and forest-green bodysuit Roy had chosen for her to wear on the trip up. Now, as she went to answer the doorbell, hatred won. When Roy frowned at her, she knew she was right.

'I know,' she said bleakly, thinking *he* looked incredibly sexy in grey trousers, grey silk shirt and a black leather jacket. 'I look awful. I just don't have big enough boobs for a bodysuit.'

'You have perfectly adequate boobs,' he said with undisguised exasperation. 'It's your hair that won't do. Take it down.'

'No,' she pouted stubbornly. 'It looks like a bush when it's out.'

'Bush is sexy.'

'I'm not sexy.'

'That's a matter of opinion. Still, have it your own way. But at least soften the look around your face with some earrings. Put on the ones you wore the other night. And darken up that lipstick a bit.'

'Good grief,' she grumbled. 'Do you do this to all your clients? Surely, since I'm paying, I can look exactly as I want to look!'

When she glared at him, he glared right back. 'I thought you wanted to throw off that stuffy old Kate this weekend,' he pointed out firmly. 'I thought you wanted to shake up your family's perception of you. I thought you wanted to knock 'em dead!'

'I *do*!'

'Then do as I say, woman, and stop quibbling!'

'All right, all right!' Kate threw her hands up in the air in defeat. The man was not only bossy and arrogant, but irritatingly right most of the time. 'You'd better come inside, then,' she muttered. 'God knows when I'm going to be ready at this rate.'

Kate's flat was not in Roy's league, but it was a nice, neat little one-bedroomed place that she had stamped her personal taste upon. She'd always liked a simple uncluttered look and colours that were restful, mostly greens and blues and greys. The rooms reflected this, and she was proud of them.

'I really like your place, Kate,' he called after her as she marched into her bedroom. 'It's like you. Classy.'

Kate wished she could hide the pleasure his compliment gave her, but she didn't have enough experience with approval to resist its pull. Her best defence against Roy's charm should have been to maintain a cool-faced composure, but she came out of her bedroom, gold dangly earrings in place, smiling broadly. 'Thank you. I like it myself. Do I look better now?'

If his eyes were lying, then he was a very good liar, she thought, her inner confidence soaring.

'Kate,' he began, the intensity he put into her name startling her, 'I . . .' He stopped, a frown drawing his straight black brows together.

She took a step forward, feeling a most peculiar panic. 'What is it?' she asked warily. 'I hope you're not going to say anything I won't want to hear.'

His smile was slow and wry. 'That would depend, I suppose.'

Again, he gave her a long, hard look before he emitted a frustrated-sounding sigh. 'The thing is, I'd rather not take your car this weekend. It would look better if we didn't, for one thing. What kind of man uses his girlfriend's car? I've managed to get myself some wheels, so if you don't mind——'

'What kind of car is it?' she demanded to know, not wanting to show up at her parents' place in a wildly painted hot-rod. 'Is it reliable?'

'Come to the window and see for yourself.'

She did, gasping when she saw the sleek silver car sitting at the kerb below. 'My God, that's a Mercedes Sports!'

'So? You have something against German cars?'

She whirled. 'No, only expensive ones! I sincerely hope that car isn't to be one of the expenses I'm expected to pay for, because if it is we'll take mine. Where on earth did you get it from, anyway? Or shouldn't I ask? Was it a little gift, perhaps, from one of your ever so grateful lady-friends? Lord knows what you had to do for it!'

Roy's face darkened for a moment. But then he smiled that slow, sardonic smile he sometimes used. 'I merely made a telephone call, my love. It belongs to Ned. He let me borrow it for the weekend.'

'Oh... Oh, I see.' Kate appreciated that she had no right to be offended or put out, even if the car had been a gift from a woman. She was hardly an innocent party since she'd hired him herself. 'Well, that's all right, then,' she said with grudging consent.

'I'm so glad you approve,' he said drily. 'Are you ready now?'

'I...I just have to take Pippa next door.'

'Who or what is Pippa?'

'My canary.'

'Ah... You do have a secret vice, then. You're a canary lover.''

His grin was so engaging that she found herself grinning back at him. Heavens, but the man was so dangerously attractive that she would give him a damned Mercedes herself, if she had one.

'Guilty as charged,' she quipped, thinking ruefully that guilt was going to be an ongoing feeling this weekend. She'd told little white lies before today, but had never attempted deception on such a grand scale. Would her family accept that a man like Roy would be her boyfriend? She was grateful now that he'd insisted on smartening up her appearance, otherwise her mother for one would never believe his interest in her was genuine.

Roy followed her while she went into the kitchen and lifted the cage down. 'Here, let me help,' he offered, taking the cage from her. 'She's a pretty little thing, isn't she? A friend of mine had a cockatoo once. Used to do tricks. Just loved lying on the bottom of his cage with his feet up in the air, pretending to be dead.'

Kate laughed. 'I don't believe you.'

'True. Cross my heart and hope to die. Unfortunately, one day he was really dead. None of us could believe it. We thought he was playing. Later, we found out some rotten kid down the street had killed him as a joke.'

'Oh, Roy, how cruel.'

'Kids *are* cruel.'

'Yes . . . yes, they are,' she murmured, old memories flashing back to haunt her.

'Hey, don't go getting all down in the mouth on me. You're all grown-up now, Kate. Whatever happened to you as a kid in the past is just that. Past. You're an adult now. Life is an empty book in front of you and it's up to you and you alone what goes in it. No one can write your story but you. No one can make your choices but you can. And no one can make you do anything you don't want to do.'

She stared at him, liking very much the philosophy he'd just expounded, especially that last part. No one could make her do anything she didn't want to do, including Roy himself.

Her smile of relief was dazzling. 'You're right!'

'Of course I'm right. Too bad it took me twenty-eight years to discover those little pearls of wisdom for myself, though.'

'T...twenty-eight years?' she said, taken aback. 'You're twenty-*eight*?'

'Yep. And next month I'll be twenty-nine. Why, did you think I was older? I probably look older. I've been burning the candle a bit at both ends lately.'

Kate was torn between being thrilled that he was only one year younger than herself and dismayed at the reminder of exactly what candle he'd been burning.

'Actually,' she said tightly, 'you look younger.'

'Do I? Great! Must be all the exercise I've been having.'

'Roy, for pity's sake!' she flared. 'Have some decorum! I'd like to *forget* what you do for a living, not have constant reminders!'

He blinked amazement at her for a second before adopting a suitably chastened expression. Though she could have sworn his mumbled apology was just this side of a chuckle. Truly, did he have no conscience at all?

'I'll take Pippa next door,' she said sharply, snatching the cage from him. 'God knows how long my neighbour will want to chat if *you* go with me.'

She stalked off with the bird, thinking to herself that if boxers had their fists declared lethal weapons then men like Roy should have certain other parts of their anatomy similarly classified.

'I'll put your luggage in the car,' he called after her. 'You lock up and meet me down there. And don't be long. Armidale is hardly around the next corner, you know.'

Which it wasn't. It was, in fact, a good eight-hour drive from Sydney up the New England highway, but it didn't take long for Kate to realise that Roy was trying to make it in record time.

'I assured my mother I would drive carefully,' she told him after he zipped across the Hawkesbury Bridge without touching the ground. 'Would you mind slowing down a little?'

'I'm only doing—— Whoops! I didn't realise I was driving this fast. This car goes like greased lightning, doesn't it?'

'It certainly does with you behind the wheel,' she said with dry reproach.

He grinned over at her. 'Speaking of your mother, did you decide to call and tell her you were bringing a friend? Or am I to be a surprise?'

'I think shock would be a better word. No, I didn't ring her.'

Kate didn't add that she had actually dialled her mother a couple of times, but on each occasion her courage had failed her.

'You might prove to be a bit of a shock yourself,' Roy stated blithely, 'looking the way you do today.'

'I'm not *that* different, surely?'

'Wait till they see you tonight. By the way, I bought you a little something, and, before you say anything, no, it won't be going on my expense list. It's in the glove box.'

'What...what is it?' she asked warily, not sure how to take Roy buying her a present. Why would he do such a thing?

'Take a look,' he said. 'It won't bite.'

She opened the glove box to find two small plastic shopping-bags.

'The one on the right,' he said. 'I didn't have time to wrap it up properly. I hope you like it.'

'Perfume!' Kate exclaimed on extracting the box of Opium.

'I noticed you didn't wear any, and I like my women smelling exotic.'

Kate stiffened. 'Maybe so, but I'm not one of your women, am I?'

His sideways glance would have driven a rivet into solid steel. 'Not yet. Now look, Kate, I think this has gone on long enough. I'm——'

'Not *ever*,' she cut in savagely. 'Do you hear me? Not ever!' And, stuffing the perfume back into its packaging, she went to ram it back into the open glove box, when her shaking hands knocked the other shopping-bag out on to her lap, spilling its contents. She stared down at the scattered business cards for several seconds before picking one up.

THE BODY BEAUTIFUL, it read. Nothing else, except three telephone numbers down in the right-hand corner. One of them was Roy's.

'Are...are these yours?' she asked, swallowing the bile that was rising in her throat. It was one thing to know how Roy was making ends meet, quite another to see the evidence with her own eyes. THE BODY BEAUTIFUL... Well, he was that all right.

'Yes,' he confessed. 'I picked them up this morning. Look, that was what I was trying to tell you about a

moment ago, Kate. Ned and I are starting up a legit-
imate business. We've bought a chain of gymnasiums
that were very run down and we've been working night
and day fixing them up for a grand opening next
weekend.'

'You mean you're going to be giving up the escort
business?' she asked with a surge of hope.

'Oh, for pity's sake!' he muttered irritably.

The penny dropped immediately. Why would he
give up such a lucrative sideline? Owning a gym would
be the perfect place to meet the sort of women he
catered for—rich, bored, neglected wives and body-
conscious career women.

'Forgive me for being so naïve,' she went on with
an acid edge. 'THE BODY BEAUTIFUL will come
in handy, won't it? A business card with a double
meaning, as well as a steady supply of potential cus-
tomers. You certainly won't have to go round picking
them up in parks!'

'My God, you're really something, aren't you? So
determined to believe I couldn't possibly have found
you an interesting and desirable woman that morning.
I had to have an ulterior motive for wanting to see
you again, for asking you out. I couldn't simply want
to be with you, or simply *want* you.'

She gave a dry laugh. 'Certainly not the way I was
looking *that* morning.'

He shook his head. 'You would have to be the most
warped female I've ever encountered.'

'I am *not* warped.'

'Yes, you are. But I aim to unwarp you.'

'Do you, now?'

'Yes, ma'am, you'd better believe it.'

'And how do you aim to do that?'

'By age-old methods.'

'Such as?'

'First I'm going to psychoanalyse you. Then I'm going to counsel you. And when that fails...' his smile carried a wicked determination '...I'm going to revert to even *older* methods.'

She had no doubt what those older methods were. His eyes were very revealing, but his arrogant presumption rekindled her spirit, and her pride.

'You told me no one could make me do anything I didn't want to do,' she pointed out archly.

'In that case, I shouldn't have any trouble.'

Though colouring, she lifted her chin, determined not to let him get the better of her. 'What about your rule of no sex on a first date?'

'Ah, but I have remembered since then that this is not our first date.'

'How convenient.'

'I agree.'

'Maybe you won't be so keen when and if it ever comes to the real thing.'

'Keen? I'm like a greyhound, straining on the leash.'

'That desperate, huh?' she scorned. 'Poor Roy. Are you going to say you love me as well?'

'Do I have to?'

'Some men will do and say anything to zero in for the kill.'

'Wow, that joker really did a good job on you, didn't he? Who was he, Kate? What did he do to make you so bitter?'

Kate turned her face away to stare out of her window. So here it came—the psychoanalysis. Her insides started squeezing tight, as they did whenever she thought of Trevor.

'Well?' Roy persisted. 'What was his name?'

'Trevor,' she bit out.

'And where did you meet him?'

'At university.'

Roy whistled. 'That long ago, eh?'

'Mmm.'

'Looks like I came along just in time, then. So what did he do?'

'I wouldn't put all the blame on Trevor. He was merely the last straw.'

'Elaborate, please.'

'I overheard him advising all his mates that I was a sure thing because I was ugly. To use his exact words, he said, "Ugly birds are always dying for it".'

'But you're not ugly, Kate. Far from it. And that is *not* flattery.'

Her laugh was bitter. 'You didn't see me back then. I wore glasses and had the worst teeth. I'd inherited my father's big teeth and my mother's small jaw, and the older I got the worse they became, all crooked and sticking out.'

'But why didn't you have them fixed as a teenager? Didn't your family have enough money? I know braces are expensive, but still...'

Kate sighed. 'They had enough money. Dad's a professor of mathemetics at the Armidale University. I guess it was my fault in a way. I was already shy about wearing glasses, and I didn't want braces as well. To begin with my teeth weren't too bad, but as time went on they just kept on getting worse.'

'Your parents should have insisted. Decisions like that aren't left up to children! Good God, what child would ever voluntarily go to a dentist?'

'Yes, I suppose so, but Dad isn't into looks and Mum had written me off as a bluestocking. She said once that she supposed a girl couldn't have looks *and* brains.'

Roy darted her an incredulous look. 'What a stupid thing to say to a sensitive and vulnerable teenage girl!'

Kate shrugged. 'Mum never understood me. She's one of those women who thinks a girl's only role in life is to look pretty, get married, and have equally pretty daughters and smart, handsome sons. Sons are allowed to be smart as well. They have different rules from daughters.'

Roy shook his head. 'And I thought I had it tough being poor. At least I always had Dad's love and approval.'

'Oh, Mum loves me. She just doesn't know what to do with me because I don't fit into that nice easy pigeon-hole she had marked out for her daughter.'

'I presume you finally had your teeth fixed yourself?'

'Yes, but it was a long and uncomfortable process. I had to have a few teeth removed first so that the others could be made to fit my small jaw.'

'Whoever did the job was good.'

'Oh, he was good all right, but damned expensive. You could go round the world a couple of times with the money I spent on my mouth.'

'I'll remember that next time I kiss it.'

Kate's stomach turned right over. She suddenly found something very interesting to examine through the side-window.

'And the glasses?' Roy went on doggedly. 'What happened to those? I suppose you changed to contact lenses.'

Now she turned to face him, having got herself under control. 'Actually, no. I had that new laser treatment for long-sighted people and I don't have to wear glasses at all any more.'

'Which is just as well,' he said. 'For you have very lovely eyes. And that's not flattery, so don't blow your stack at me.'

'Oh, I won't do that. I've decided you can flatter me all you like this weekend. I'm going to lap it up. After all, I'm paying for the privilege. But there will be no sex in any circumstances, so I suggest you stick to flattery. In fact, say some more outrageously flattering things so I can get used to them.'

His laughter was infectious. 'All right. You're the boss. Well, did you know you have a very sexy voice? It's kinda soft and low and on the phone it sends shivers right down to my—er...'

'Toes?' she suggested drily.

'That's it! And then... *then*, there's your tushy.'

'*Tushy*?'

'You know.' And, leaning forward over the steering-wheel, he made the motion to smack himself on the buttocks. 'Haven't you heard of that word? It's one of the more polite terms. Well, anyway, you do have a nice one, Kate. It's kinda pokey-out but firm and real cute, and when it wiggles, my, oh, my, does it give a fella some *bad* thoughts.'

Roy had made Kate blush once or twice since they'd met, but this time the heat seemed to radiate from deep inside, fanning up through her stomach and chest till it hit her face with the force of a blast-furnace.

She gave a small moan of distress, which sent those beautiful blue eyes of his whipping round to witness her embarrassment.

'Oh-oh, I've embarrassed you again. Look, just forget I said that, Kate. Next time I'll keep my compliments for bits above the waist. No, scratch that out as well. Above the neck.' His gaze landed on her parted lips. 'Nope, that could be dangerous too. We shall concentrate on your intellectual capabilities, which I am sure far surpass mine, so we won't talk about them either.' He heaved a frustrated sigh. 'Having exhausted my supply of non-embarrassing flattery, I'll turn the conversation over to yours truly.'

A totally flustered Kate threw her hands up in the air in defeat before starting to giggle. For it was all too ridiculous for words, the whole situation.

'Ah, now *that's* what we could talk about,' he said, sounding pleased with himself. 'Your delightful sense of humour. Tell me, Kate, do you like Woody Allen movies?'

'Can't stand a bar of them,' she admitted laughingly.

'Thank God! I was beginning to think I was the only one. And do you like slapstick?'

'Hate it.'

'This is getting better and better.'

'So what was your favourite comedy series of all time on television?'

'Let's see...it's...no...it's...oh, I just can't make up my mind between *Father Dear Father* and *Butterflies*.'

'Extraordinary!'

'Why?'

'I've never heard of either of them.'

'Good lord, where have you been all your life?'

'Playing football?'

'You can't play football all day, every day.'

'Yes, well I reserved my nights for other activities.'
Kate threw him a dry look.

His grimace was one of mock-dismay. 'Delete that!
I watched reruns of *Yes, Minister*.'

'Ah, now that was a good show. Is it your
favourite?'

'Nope.'

'What, then?' she asked with an expressive sigh.

'It's a toss-up between *'Allo, 'Allo* and *MASH*.'

'You're into war, then, are you?'

'Of course. I'm a man!'

'Ah, that you are, Roy. That you are.'

'Was that a compliment?'

'No, flattery.'

His chuckle was highly amused. 'She's learning. By
George, she's learning.'

'Given enough time with you, I dare say a girl would
learn quite a lot, most of which she wouldn't want
her mother to witness.'

'Kate Reynolds! That's not a very flattering thing
to say. Are you suggesting your virtue might be com-
promised this weekend?'

'Not in the least. I have my mother on tap to
chaperon proceedings. If you think you're going to
sneak into my bedroom after hours, then think again.
My room is next to my parents', and Mum has ears
like the submarine sonar operator in *The Hunt For
Red October*.'

Kate almost gasped when Roy shot her a truly
shocked look. 'Don't tell me you've read Tom
Clancy!'

'Read him and liked him. Why?'

'He's my all-time favourite author!'

'He's not mine.'

'Roy's face fell. 'Oh ... pity ...'

'I like Stephen King better.'

Now his eyes lit up like lighthouse beacons. 'He's my second. Gee, Kate, for a minute there I thought we didn't agree on something.'

'I'm sure there are many things we don't agree upon.'

'One of them being your decision that sex is out this weekend.'

'Not just this weekend,' she said curtly, teeth clenching hard in her jaw.

'I won't charge you extra.'

'How kind of you.'

'You're losing your sense of humour again.'

'No, I'm not. I'm just making sure you understand the situation.'

'Oh, I understand the situation, Kate,' he said in a voice that carried a surprising seriousness. 'I'm understanding it better all the time.'

He fell silent then, and so did she.

The road whizzed by, the Mercedes eating up the miles. The Hunter Valley came and went, and eventually the Northern Tablelands were upon them. They had only stopped once, at Muswellbrook, to eat and go to the toilet, after which Roy had really put his foot down, relegating their spasmodic conversation to the most banal topics.

When a signpost told them Armidale was a mere twenty kilometres off, a type of tension invaded the car. Or was it just Kate who felt tense, nervous over what her parents would say when they saw she had brought a man home for the first time in her life? Not any man, either. A young, handsome, sexy hunk of a man.

Or was she worried over what secret plans Roy might be hatching within that ruthless mind of his? For he *was* ruthless. No way did she believe his claim that he'd been attracted to her from the start, that he'd asked her out because he'd wanted her for himself. That was a lie.

Oh, she didn't doubt that he'd grown to like her a little since then. There was a definite rapport between them on an intellectual level, a communion of spirit, but she would never swallow his flattery about desiring her physically. Possibly his ego had been challenged by her refusing to go to bed with him, and so he was determined to seduce her. Or maybe his subtle sexual threats and promises were designed to get her so intrigued and fascinated by him that she would be willing to pay for that little extra.

Kate could not see herself ever doing such a scandalous thing, but she had to admit that her assertion that she would not sleep with him was nothing but one last desperate defence against the mad desires he kept engendering within her. She knew—as she suspected he did as well—that he would only have to start making love to her and she would not make him stop.

The thought both terrified and enthralled her.

CHAPTER EIGHT

'IT's years since I've been to Armidale,' Roy said as they entered the large country town. 'But it's as pretty as I remember.'

Kate glanced around with new eyes. When a place was home, sometimes you forgot to really look at it. Now she took in the lovely old homes and churches, the English-style gardens, and the splendid trees, most of whose leaves were russet and gold now that autumn was half over.

'Yes, it's a pretty town,' she agreed. 'But darned cold in the winter.'

'I suspect it's not too warm out there today, despite the sun. But then it's after four. You'd better give me directions, madam, or we'll end up on our way to Brisbane.'

'What? Oh, right, well, don't turn left here, go straight ahead. Then up that hill, turn right on the crest, and we're the third place along on the right. Number six. It's an old federation-style house complete with enclosed front porch and stained-glass windows.'

'Sounds charming.'

'What? Oh, yes . . . yes, I suppose it is.'

'You're a bundle of nerves, aren't you?'

'I'll be better once we get the introductions over.'

'Shouldn't you have perhaps told me a little more about your family?'

She shot him a startled look. 'Golly, yes, I didn't think of that.'

He slid the Mercedes over to the kerb under a large elm and stopped the engine. 'A few more minutes won't hurt. I think I should at least know your brothers' names, along with their wives. Forget the children. I'll never remember them, anyway. OK, shoot!'

'My oldest brother is Jeff. His wife's Dawn. Then there's Bevan, married to Loretta.'

'What about your father and mother?'

'You'd better call them Mr and Mrs Reynolds. They're rather old-fashioned.'

'Yeah, but I'm not. Give me their names, Kate, and leave that up to me.'

Kate sighed, thinking to herself that this just wasn't going to work. None of it. 'Dad's Henry and Mum's Alice.'

'Does your father drink?'

She blinked her astonishment. 'Well, he's not a tee-totaller, but he's not a drunk, either.'

'Don't be so defensive! I was simply trying to find out whether I should present the box of booze I have in the boot as my contribution to the barbecue.'

'If I say yes, will I get billed for it?'

Roy laughed. 'Of course. You can't expect me to give you *everything* for nothing!'

'I don't expect you to give me *anything* for nothing,' she snapped. 'If you like, you can bill me for the perfume as well.'

His expression carried exasperation. 'Oh, Kate... Whatever am I going to do with you?'

'Nothing, I hope,' she bit out. 'Now, about the booze. Is it beer?'

'Yes, plus a couple of bottles of specially selected white wine just for you.'

'Specially selected? What does that mean?'

His smile was mischievous. 'It means I studied the alcoholic content and picked the ones with the highest percentage.'

Kate folded her arms and gave him a droll look. 'Do you honestly think getting me drunk will help your cause in getting me into bed? Let me assure you, that won't work.'

'And let me assure you, Kate Reynolds, that my choice of wine had nothing to do with seduction. I simply thought you might need some Dutch courage to stand by my side and be a convincing fallen woman.'

She stiffened, her arms unfolding, her back straightening. 'What...what do you mean—fallen woman?'

'Well, you don't expect people to believe we *aren't* sleeping together, do you? Let's face it, Kate, girls of your age only bring two types of men home to meet their family. Fiancés and lovers. Since I'm definitely not your fiancé, then it's only logical they will conclude I'm your lover. Moving on from there, if I'm *your* lover, then you're *my* lover, and I tell you, Kate, when a woman's my lover I don't stand ten feet away from her on a Saturday night. In fact, I don't park at a kerb with her without doing something like this...'

When one was strapped into the front passenger seat of a car with the belt firmly in place, it really was difficult to stop the driver from kissing you, especially if somewhere along the line he had sneakily undone his own belt, and especially if you'd been dying for that man to kiss you for days.

Kate made no pretence at fighting Roy's marauding mouth. Perhaps she did freeze for a split second with the sheer unexpectedness of his move, but from the moment those firm, warm lips started feasting on hers as if he was starving for the taste of her, she was, as she had prophesied, a goner.

'Oh, Kate . . . Kate,' he groaned between their first two kisses, the passion in his voice overwhelming her. On the third kiss, his tongue entered the fray and all hell broke loose. It felt so *different* from that time back in front of the lift at work. So incredibly different.

Back then, her response to such an unexpected, alien intimacy had perhaps been more shock than anything. This time, however, Kate was galvanised by the feel of that tongue filling her mouth. She exulted in its driving desire, in the explosive tension of Roy's hands about her face, in the press of his strong male fingers as they splayed up into her hair. The sudden and awe-inspiring possibility that this man really wanted her was more intoxicating than the most potent wine. He couldn't be putting on such passion, could he? Oh, surely not . . .

Kate didn't think about it for too long, simply because she stopped thinking all round.

Soft, sensual moans started a low echo in her throat. Her hands came up between them to rest at the base of his throat, her fingertips trembling as they moved down the slightly hair-roughened V of his open-necked shirt. A blind raw need for more of his flesh to explore had her fumbling with the buttons on his shirt.

When his hands suddenly closed over hers and that hungry mouth abruptly withdrew, she blinked up at him. Roy's expression was rueful as he pressed her hands down on to her lap and fell back into his seat.

'I'd really like this to continue, Kate, but, given the time and the place, I must call a halt. So please stop looking at me like that...' Leaning back over, he placed a gentle hand on to her flushed cheek, his eyes caressing as they travelled slowly over her swollen mouth. 'I'm sorry, honey. This is as hard for me as it is for you...'

Now that the moment of madness was over, Kate was quietly appalled at how quickly she'd been reduced to a compulsively sensual creature, and how quickly she was willing to believe anything. As if Roy really wanted her. His kissing her was just another clever move to remind her of what she could have if she was willing to pay for it.

She groaned at the memory of her hands fumbling with his shirt as though she couldn't get enough of him. Maybe Trevor had been right about her, she agonised. Maybe women like her didn't have any control or common sense when it came to sex. They were so frustrated, so pent-up from never having experienced its release, that they simply went off their heads with wanting and need.

Roy was still leaning over her, smiling down into her wide green eyes with a seductive heavy-lidded gaze. When his fingertips brushed over her bottom lip she sucked in a startled gasp, amazed that such a simple caress could so quickly rekindle the fires his earlier kisses had ignited so explosively.

'You do have a lovely mouth,' he murmured.

Kate clamped her teeth hard in her jaw. 'Roy, stop it,' she bit out.

His eyes narrowed with exasperation. 'When are you going to learn how to take a compliment?'

'When it's genuine,' she snapped. 'Do you really think you can fool me with a couple of kisses and some feigned passion? I told you once and I'll tell you again: I'm not about to pay for sex, no matter how good at it you think you are. Why don't you get that through your head?'

His fury was immediate and violent. 'Feigned passion!' he grated out, and, snatching up her hand, drew it forcibly into his lap. 'Does that feel like feigned passion to you?'

With a frustrated growl, he threw her hand back. 'God, I've never come across a woman like you. I'll bet I could rave on here for hours, explaining, exhorting, excusing, and you still wouldn't believe what I was saying. But I'm going to say it anyway. I want you, Kate Reynolds, as a man wants a woman. No frills, no garbage. Just that. Take it or leave it!'

'Then I'll leave it, thanks! All I want from you, Roy Fitzsimmons, is what I'm paying for.'

'And that's all you'll damned well get, too!' Firing the engine, he accelerated angrily on up the street. 'Right on the crest,' he muttered. 'Then third on the right. Right?'

'Right.'

Kate slanted a frowning glance over at Roy's furious face. His anger was an ally, she realised with a degree of surprise. For there had been nothing feigned in what had lain beneath her hand. He *had* wanted her at that moment, maybe as much as she had wanted him. Which just showed how dangerous he was. Clearly, he was a very virile, highly sexed man, who didn't need a beautiful young woman in his arms to become turned on. Any woman would do, apparently, herself included.

A shudder ran through her, bringing a sharp look from Roy. Their eyes clashed, and, whatever it was that he saw behind her wide-eyed gaze, it made his anger fade. 'Maybe the wine will make you more amenable,' he remarked somewhat ruefully. 'I'll try again later.'

'Try what again?' she demanded with a dark, panicky churning in her stomach.

'To make you listen, my love. And to make you understand my motives.'

'I think I understand your motives quite well already.'

'Oh, no. You haven't even begun to understand. But you will . . . in time. Is that your mother coming out to greet us?'

Kate's eyes swung from Roy to the figure coming down the front steps of her parents' home.

'Oh, my God,' she muttered under her breath as Roy slid the silver car into the kerb and turned off the engine, her eyes never leaving her mother.

Alice Reynolds was one of those women who would never be seen dead in anything but a dress. Luckily, her husband, Henry, was one of those men who preferred things that way. He denigrated jeans as unfeminine, often saying with disparagement that if women could see what they looked like from behind they wouldn't wear them. Clearly, he and Roy were not on the same wavelength, for Kate suspected that viewing women in tight trousers from behind was one of Roy's favourite occupations. Which explained what she was wearing at the moment.

Kate swallowed at the thought of what her mother's comment would be about her clothes. Odd that at this moment her worries should be directed towards her appearance, instead of the man sitting behind the steering-wheel. Yet she supposed her mother's disapproval of her made-over self might transfer to disapproval of Kate's pretend relationship with Roy.

The woman herself was bearing down on them at the moment, wearing pale blue and pearls, a bewildered frown the only minus on her perfectly made-up face. Though nearing sixty, she looked no more than forty-five, with her short curly hair carefully blonded and her far from matronly figure kept slender with daily walking.

'*Kate*?' She peered across the front gate through the passenger window of the Mercedes.

Kate decided to take the bull by the horns, jumping out of the car and flashing her mother a disarming grin. 'Yes, it's me.' She bounced over and gave her astonished mother a kiss on the cheek. 'I hope you don't mind, but I've brought a friend with me after all. And no, I haven't won a lottery. That's his car, not mine.'

As though on cue, Roy came striding round the front of the Mercedes at this point in time, a broad smile on his face.

'Hi, there,' he said breezily. 'I'm Roy, Kate's friend. So tell me, are you Dawn or Loretta?'

Kate rolled her eyes at him, knowing darned well he knew this was her mother. But the outrageous flattery worked like a charm, the outcome being that Kate's figure-hugging clothes didn't rate a second glance, let alone criticism. Her mother was far too busy staring at Roy and preening at his compliment at the same time.

'I'm neither,' she corrected sweetly. 'I'm Kate's mother. But you can call me Alice.' And she held out her beautifully manicured hand.

Roy covered it with both of his. 'How kind of you to make me feel so welcome. I do hope I won't be intruding on your family occasion.'

'Oh, no! We've been on at Kate to bring a friend to these weekends for years. Her father will be delighted, as will both her brothers.'

Kate watched the scene with a rueful resignation. She should have known that she wouldn't be the only female Roy could take by storm. No doubt Dawn and Loretta would be eating out of his hands in no time as well, as would their little girls.

'Come in, come in,' her mother said, hurrying to open the gate for them.

'We'd better get the luggage first, Mum. When are the others due?'

'Oh, not for a couple of hours. And it's only the adults tonight. Jeff and his lot are staying with Bevan and Loretta for the night and they've hired a joint baby-sitter. Just as well they didn't change their mind and stay here, since I'll be needing the guest room for your Roy.'

Kate gave *her* Roy a sickly smile.

'Don't go to any trouble for me, Alice,' he said gallantly. 'I can bunk anywhere.'

'I can't see you fitting on the sofa, young man.'

'I could always bunk in with the daughter of the house,' he whispered to Kate while their heads were together in the car boot.

'It's a single bed,' she returned drily.

'That's OK. I'm liberated. You can be on top.'

Kate glared at him. 'Is that supposed to be funny?'

Roy sighed. 'I just wanted to hear you laugh, honey. You're too uptight. Relax. Everything's going to be fine.'

And amazingly, it was. Her father took to Roy as quickly as her mother had, though of course he had, as opposed to Alice, immediately recognised Roy as the famous sportsman he was. Kate was gratified, and considerably surprised, that both her parents seemed to readily accept their supposed relationship. Her mother particularly seemed delighted, cornering her by herself as soon as she could.

'Kate, wherever did you meet that heart-throb of a man?' she asked, closing Kate's bedroom door behind her. 'And why didn't you tell me about him earlier in the week when I rang?'

Kate wished she and Roy had compared stories, though from her mother's questions he hadn't told her much about their history. She decided to stick fairly close to the truth, though she thought it best to expand the time since their first meeting.

'I didn't think I'd be able to persuade him to come,' she said lightly, hiding any guilt at lying by setting out her new make-up and perfume on her old dressing-table. 'He's been very busy starting up a new business.'

'Oh, yes, I heard him telling Henry about that. Something to do with gymnasiums.'

'That's right,' she said, her heart squeezing tight when she thought of all the women he'd meet at those gyms.

'Yes, but where did you *meet* him?' her mother persisted, sitting down on the side of the bed and looking as if she was settling in for a long inquisition.

'Meet him?' Kate gulped, turned round, and smiled what she hoped was an innocent-looking smile. 'I— er—ran into him in the park one morning and we got talking.'

'Ran into him? Oh, you mean you've taken up jogging. I did notice how trim you were looking. But isn't that a bit dangerous, letting a man pick you up like that?'

'I did recognise him, Mum. He's very famous down Sydney way.'

'Is he *really*? Henry said he was, but I know nothing about sport. Have you been going out together for long?'

'Not too long,' Kate hedged, picking up the bottle of Opium and idly running her fingers up and down the bottle.

'Did Roy give you that?' Alice asked with a frown in her voice.

Kate's hand tightened around the bottle. She'd been waiting for the disapproval, and no doubt here it was. 'Yes, why?' she said sharply. 'Is there something wrong with a man giving a girl perfume?'

'There's no need to snap, Kate,' her mother returned just as sharply. 'I was merely making small talk, like mothers and daughters usually do. I know you've never liked that sort of thing in the past, but you seemed different this weekend and I was hoping that, in the circumstances, you might have changed.'

'Why? Because I've brought a man home at long last?' she lashed out, all the old hurts rising up to take voice. 'Can I hope for your approval now that I've shown I can attract a man as well as even the prettiest girl? That *is* the only measure of success for a daughter where you're concerned, isn't it?'

Her mother sighed and stood up. 'I'm sorry if you think that, Kate. I do believe most women are not completely happy without a man by their side, but I appreciate there are certain women in this world who prefer their career to a husband and children. But you're not of them, my dear. You never have been.'

Something exploded inside Kate. 'Don't tell me what I am or what I never was or what I will be! How would you know? You know nothing about me!'

Alice stared at her daughter before shaking her head, her shoulders sagging. 'Oh, Kate... Do you still hold that one thoughtless comment against me? I was trying to make you feel better about yourself that day, but it came out all wrong. Yet because of it you've hated me ever since, haven't you?'

Kate was appalled when her mother started to cry, the heart-rending sobs tearing at her insides. She raced forward, disgusted with herself. How could she have been so cruel and heartless? Hadn't she always known that her mother loved her, that she just hadn't known how to handle her introverted, difficult daughter? Kate remembered the tantrum she'd put on when her mother had made an appointment for her at the dentist's when she was fourteen. She'd cried and cried, insisting she was happy with her teeth the way they were.

How was her mother to know she'd been more afraid of boys teasing her over braces than she had been embarrassed by her teeth? Then later, when her teeth had worsened, she'd always refused to discuss them, for by then she'd believed the problem insurmountable. It was only many years later, when she'd read an article in a magazine about new orthodontic methods, that she'd plucked up the courage to do something about them.

Like scales falling from her eyes, she saw that most of her problems had been of her own making, yet she'd always blamed her mother, and here she was, still using the poor woman as her whipping-boy.

'Oh, Mum . . . Mum, I don't hate you,' she cried, hugging the weeping woman and trying not to cry herself. 'I love you. It's just that I've been so unhappy and lonely for so long, and I thought . . . I thought . . .'

'That I might not approve of your Roy?' Alice sniffed, wiping her nose with one of those lacy linen handkerchiefs she always seemed to have with her.

'Something like that,' Kate lied with a weak sigh of relief. She should have known that her mother's tears would go as quickly as they had come. But the brief rush of emotion had had a wonderfully cleansing effect on her own soul. That old dark bitterness had gone. Forever.

'Why?' Alice asked. 'Because you're sleeping with him?'

Kate choked out an astonished laugh. 'Roy said you'd think that.'

'And you're not?' Her mother was clearly surprised, which showed she was not as old-fashioned as Kate had always thought.

'No. We're just good friends.'

Alice's look was sceptical. 'That's not the impression he gave me.'

'Oh? What did he say?'

'Nothing really. It was just an impression.'

'He wants to sleep with me,' she blurted out, knowing she was twisting the truth, but desperately wanting her mother to believe that Roy found her really desirable. Or was it herself she was trying to convince? If only he *did* want her as she'd always wanted to be wanted. No, *needed* to be wanted.

'And you, Kate?' her mother asked quietly. 'What do you want?'

She flushed fiercely.

'I see . . . Well, do be careful, dear. There are worse things that can happen to a girl these days than an unwanted pregnancy.'

She stared at her mother. For she'd not allowed her mind to go that far, to accept that she might actually end up in bed with Roy. It demonstrated the many dangers inherent in lusting after a man like him. 'I...I didn't think of that,' she admitted.

'Well, I think you should. A man like Roy won't have been hiding his light under a bushel, so to speak.'

'You can say that again,' Kate muttered under her breath.

'Are you going to change for the barbecue or wear what you've got on?'

Kate flinched at the thought of the leather outfit. 'I'm not sure.'

'Your father doesn't like trousers, you know. Not that what you've got on doesn't suit you. It really does. You look very smart.'

Kate smiled. This compliment, she knew, was genuine. If her mother hadn't liked how she looked, she would have simply said nothing. 'Thank you,' Kate said happily.

Now her mother smiled, and Kate had never felt so warmed. If nothing else, she would be grateful to Roy for this.

'Shall we go downstairs and have a sherry together while I cut up some salad?' her mother suggested.

'You can have a sherry. I'm going to open a bottle of the white wine Roy brought specially for me.'

'Sounds as if that man's been buying a lot of things specially for you,' Alice remarked thoughtfully as they left the room.

CHAPTER NINE

A COUPLE of years previously, Kate's mother and father had had their small back porch extended into a large sheltered family area with plenty of comfy outdoor furniture and an enormous coal-burning barbecue. This latter cooked the most delicious meat, as well as providing enough heat to stop guests from feeling too chilled, even on a cool April evening.

When Alice and Kate came downstairs, Roy and Henry were out near the barbecue, claiming to be getting things ready, and indeed the fire had been started, but there seemed to be more drinking than preparing going on. A couple of bottles of Henry's favourite claret were sitting on the huge circular plastic table, and each was already at low tide.

Kate watched Roy for a while through the kitchen window. He seemed to be really enjoying himself in her father's company, chatting away happily, with bursts of intermittent laughter. No doubt her father was regaling him with all those old jokes the rest of the family had heard a dozen times. But no matter, they were probably new to Roy.

Thinking about her own father reminded Kate that Roy had lost *his* dad only recently. She had no doubts that he had loved his father very much, from the way he spoke about him, and must miss him terribly. It saddened Kate that Roy had no close family at all left alive now. Maybe if he'd had a family to care about—

and to care about him—then he wouldn't have drifted into such a soul-destroying lifestyle.

The saddest part was that maybe he didn't realise the danger yet. He was only a relatively young man. At twenty-eight, sex with lots of different women possibly seemed exciting. Being paid for it was icing on the cake. But no one could sell themselves like that and not eventually lose all self-respect. If only she could convince him that he didn't need money that badly. Why, if he put all his energies into the gyms he'd bought, she was sure he could be a big financial success. Which was what he wanted, wasn't it? Money, not sex. Or was it?

Thinking about sex in conjunction with Roy was not a good idea. He'd replaced the black leather jacket with a cream Aran sweater which hugged his shoulders and chest, showing their broad, muscular lines. Her eyes began travelling over those lines, and everything inside her tightened.

Kate was unnerved by what just looking at this man could do to her. Hopefully, she would continue to be strong enough to resist him, otherwise it might be *her* self-respect on the line at some future date, not Roy's.

'Stop standing there mooning,' her mother reprimanded. 'Either help me with these salads or go get one of the men to open a bottle of the white wine Roy brought. It's in the fridge.'

Kate took a deep breath and turned to walk over to the refrigerator, where she drew out a bottle of Riesling. 'That's a quaint old word...''mooning'',' she commented dreamily.

'Quaint, but accurate,' her mother said, giving her another incisive glance. 'You're really smitten with him, aren't you?'

Smitten ... Yes, she was smitten all right. But with what?

'I suppose I am,' she agreed.

'And how does he feel about you?'

'Oh, he likes me well enough.'

Her mother lifted an eyebrow. 'Only *likes*? I would have said his feelings were stronger than that.'

Kate gave a short, dry laugh. 'Yes, but I'm not supposed to tell my mother about that part.'

Alice frowned. 'Kate, you will be careful, won't you? I mean——'

'Yes, Mum,' she reassured her parent with a quick squeeze around the shoulders. 'I'll be very careful. Stop worrying. I'm a big girl now.' Quite deliberately, she decided to put on a bright and breezy act to distract her mother from her growing concern about Roy's intentions.

Quickly she moved over to open the back door, standing on the back steps with her hands on her hips. 'So!' she called out. 'Which one of you inebriated gentlemen is going to open a bottle of wine for the poor work-trodden women of the family?'

Roy whirled round, showing a moment's surprise at her happy-go-lucky manner. 'I'm not sure,' he said. 'What does inebriated mean? Henry, why have you raised this daughter of yours to use such big words?'

'Don't look at me. She never takes any notice of anything I say. Just look at what she's wearing. Trousers! Can't stand women in trousers.'

'Neither can I.' Roy's blue eyes glittered cheekily as they locked on to Kate's. 'Your father wants you to go and take those trousers off straight away, Kate. Hop to it.'

'No trousers coming up,' she agreed, unable to resist Roy's wicked sense of humour.

Her father almost spilt his drink. 'What's that? I didn't mean . . .' He looked from Roy to his daughter, a wide smile breaking out on to his large ruddy face as they both grinned at him. 'You two were pulling my leg then, weren't you?'

'Would we do that, Dad?' Laughing, Kate came over and ruffled his thinning hair. 'How's things at the uni these days?'

'Not too bad. How's things in the big smoke?'

'Improving.'

'You earning lots of money?'

'Yep.'

'Money isn't everything, daughter.'

'That's what I keep telling her, Henry,' Roy chipped in with a straight face.

Kate threw him a disbelieving look.

'A woman her age should be widening her horizons,' he went on blithely. 'There's so much more to life other than filthy lucre. Why, there's sport, travel, babies——'

'Babies!' Kate squawked, flashing Roy a scornful glance. 'Now who's pulling whose leg?'

'Certainly not me,' Roy said so seriously that Kate was flabbergasted. Why, the man was a consummate actor. If he set his mind to it he could make a girl believe anything!

'Stop this nonsense and come and open the wine,' she reproached sharply. 'And you, Daddy, dear, stop getting plastered and start getting organised.'

'Just like her mother. Can't let a man just sit!' Henry muttered as Kate pulled Roy aside and towards the kitchen.

'I do wish you'd behave,' she hissed. 'I'm paying you to be my boyfriend, not the court jester. Babies, indeed! Kindly don't start giving my parents any permanent ideas about us. My mother already thinks you might have designs on me.'

'Smart woman.'

Kate ground to a halt, green eyes flashing. 'You're not going to start on that rubbish about really wanting me again, are you?'

'Not at this precise moment.'

'Not at *any* moment! Now just do your job, please. Smile and be a pleasant companion, but don't—I repeat, *do not*—come on too strong. The last thing I want is my family asking when the wedding bells will be ringing.'

Roy's wry smile sent a spurt of pique racing through her, finding its way rapidly to her tongue. 'God, this was a dumb idea. I've no idea why I let you talk me into it.'

'Haven't you?'

'Oh, dear lord, not more of your innuendoes! Look, give the smart repartee a rest, will you? And stick to what you do best.'

'Which is?'

'Being the hunk of the month,' she threw at him, and, whirling round, marched up the back steps. But as she went in the back door, which was part glass, she caught a glimpse of Roy's reflection just behind her. And what she saw took her aback. Never had she seen him look like that—smouldering with a dark fury.

Guilt flooded in. She had no right to be contemptuous of him when what she was doing was just as despicable. She was the one who'd hired him, after all. That made her just as bad.

Logic, however, didn't seem to soothe her own anger. Perhaps, underneath, she was distressed at how much she really liked Roy, despite everything. The lust part she could understand and forgive herself for. A lot of women would react to Roy like that. But the liking was another thing. Why was she so susceptible to his charm, and his personality? And why should the thought of never seeing him again after this weekend fill her with such dread?

It worried her that she might do something silly, just so that wouldn't happen.

'Did you get your father moving?' Alice asked, not looking up from where she was putting the finishing touches on several bowls of salad. A glass of sherry stood at her elbow, half empty. When she stopped to pick it up, she glanced up. 'Ah Roy... You're the wine-opening volunteer, are you?'

'Yes, but he's complaining,' Kate tossed off, determined not to let Roy get to her, even though having him stand close beside her was disturbing. 'Where's the opener, Mum?'

'Over there.' She pointed. 'It's time you changed, Kate, if you're still going to. But as I said earlier, you look very nice in what you're wearing. Green suits you. What do you think, Roy?'

'What do Dawn and Loretta usually wear?' he asked, and took the opener from Kate's hand.

'They always do themselves up to the nines, don't they, Kate?'

'Yes.'

'Then change,' Roy told Kate firmly. 'And leave your hair down.'

'Maybe I will and maybe I won't.' Her eyes met his, daring him to argue with her. But he merely smiled a rueful smile and kept on opening the wine. 'You'll look after Roy while I'm gone, won't you, Mum?'

'He's a big boy, dear. He doesn't need anyone to hold his hand.'

As Kate moved out of the room and up the hallway she heard Roy's soft chuckle. 'Don't tell Kate that,' he said. 'I *like* holding *her* hand.'

Kate ground to a halt, worried now over what Roy might say to her mother.

'I've no doubt you do, young man,' Alice returned crisply. 'That's because she's a very special girl. I wouldn't ever want to hear my Kate's been hurt by someone who doesn't appreciate that fact.'

Kate flushed with pleasure at her mother speaking so proudly and protectively of her. She wasn't so pleased, however, with Roy's ironic answer.

'You don't have to worry on that score, Alice. No one appreciates the woman Kate is more than me.'

Kate hurried on, green eyes blazing. So he appreciated the woman she was, did he? The mocking bastard! God, she couldn't wait to put on that leather outfit, take her hair down, drown herself in that sexy perfume, and then, once she'd turned the randy devil on, she would delight in turning him down once more.

'Good grief!' her father exclaimed when she made a reappearance. 'Is that a skirt or a wide belt? And where did you get all that hair from?'

'From you, Dad. Before it turned grey and you lost it, that is.'

'What an...interesting outfit,' her mother said with more kindness that conviction. 'And I think her hair looks very becoming, Henry.'

'Thanks, Mum.' Kate grinned, knowing exactly what her mother thought of the tan leather suit, with its short, tight skirt, body-hugging waistcoat and fringed jacket. Kate's amused grin faded when she turned to throw Roy a challenging glance. 'Aren't you going to say something complimentary as well?'

Roy was standing with her mother and father, near the heat of the barbecue. Slowly he walked towards her so that she and she alone could see the expression in his eyes. Roy had looked at her with desire when she'd tried the outfit on in the shop. But this . . . this was more than desire. This was raw passion. It stunned her. Could he summon up such looks at will, as he summoned up other parts of his body?

'You look smashing,' he said, then bent to press soft lips against her cheek. 'I wish we were alone,' he whispered while his mouth was close to her ear.

Wide green eyes flew to him as he straightened. He saw her fear and shook his head slightly, a dark frown on his face. 'I have to talk to you alone, Kate,' he murmured. 'Soon . . .'

She did not say anything, *could* not say anything. Everything inside her was still shaking from his warm breath on her face, those moist lips against her cheek. But worst was the rush of intense longing that had surged through her when he'd whispered his wish to be alone with her.

The doorbell ringing was a godsend.

'That will be the others arriving. Go and greet them, Kate,' her mother suggested. 'Show them how lovely you look. Then bring them back here to meet Roy. Roy, come and tell me some more about these gymnasiums of yours.'

If Kate hadn't been so perturbed by her encounter with Roy she might have gained much more pleasure and satisfaction from the reactions of her brothers and their wives to her new self. She was subject to everything from stunned stares and wolf-whistles from the men, to gushing compliments and breathless questioning from the women.

'Kate, is that really you?' Dawn gasped. 'Oh, but I'd *kill* to be able to wear an outfit like that! And your hair! Is that some kind of special perm? I never realised before it was so curly, or so *red*!'

'And she's so slim!' Loretta chimed in. 'Have you been dieting?'

Kate blinked at the reference to her weight. She'd always been slim, but perhaps she'd never worn clothes that showed off her figure quite so well.

'Love your hair out like that, sis,' Bevan said after he whistled a second time.

'Yeah. Lookin' good, kid,' Jeff agreed.

The reactions to her 'heart-throb' boyfriend might have been equally satisfying if Roy had been her boyfriend for real, and not some devil who was out to corrupt her. Loretta merely gaped for a full minute. Dawn appeared cool on the surface but she swooned behind Roy's back, mouthing, 'Gorgeous!' to Kate. Bevan, who was a solicitor in Armidale and had always been a football fanatic, went ape when he saw who their guest was. Jeff, a high-school science teacher at a private school in Brisbane, was not quite so familiar with Sydney footballers, though he'd certainly heard of Roy and was clearly impressed with his sister having such a handsome, intelligent boyfriend.

For Roy *was* intelligent. Kate hadn't realised just how smart he was till that evening. His general knowledge was staggering, for while her talkative family discussed topics over dinner ranging from sport to politics to music to geography to wine and even cooking, he was never at a loss for words and knew some obscure things that only a person with a quick, retentive brain could have remembered.

'You should go on one of those quiz shows,' Alice suggested to Roy over coffee. 'You have a very wide knowledge.'

'I used to read encyclopaedias when I was growing up.'

'That's rather odd material for a young lad,' Henry joined in.

Roy shrugged nonchalantly, but Kate had glimpsed a momentary flash of remembered pain. 'I was an only child with an invalid parent. I had to stay home a lot and look after Dad. My mum died when I was young, you see. When our television broke down one year we couldn't afford to have it fixed, so when I had nothing to do I read this old set of encyclo-paedias Dad had picked up cheap at a fête several years before. I found them quite interesting, actually.'

The loneliness and extreme poverty in Roy's story touched Kate.

'That's so sad,' Dawn sniffed, echoing Kate's thoughts.

'Yes, Roy,' Bevan added. 'It must have been hard on you.'

'Things weren't always as bad as that. The next year I was selected for the state under-sixteens football team. That really perked Dad up.'

Kate frowned at this last remark. It sounded as if the only reason he had played football in the first place was for his dad. It left her wondering about Roy as she'd never wondered before. What made him tick? Why did he do what he was doing? What did he want out of life, besides money?

She watched him more closely for the rest of the evening, and he saw her watching him. Every time their eyes met he would signal with his eyes for her to go inside the house, but she had already made the decision to resist being alone with Roy as much as possible. She was far too vulnerable to him, and he was far too dangerous.

Shortly after one o'clock she did have the opportunity to talk to him in relative privacy but without any risk that he would make a pass at her. Kate's brothers and their wives had just left, and Roy and Kate had offered to do the washing-up while her parents cleared up the barbecue area. With her mother and father just on the other side of the kitchen window Kate felt fairly safe.

'Did you really like playing football?' she asked, glancing over to where he was standing with a tea-towel in his hands.

His returning glance was sharp. 'That's an odd sort of question.'

Kate shrugged. 'Sometimes people do things because others expect it. Children, especially, try to make their parents proud of them. When I decided I would never be able to do that with Mum, I did my best to make Dad proud of my academic achievements. I often wonder if I would have been so good at school if I'd been pretty.'

'I'm sure you would have. You're exceptionally bright. And you're right about me and football. It was more for Dad than for myself. I would never have given up my law degree in normal circumstances, but at the time I thought Dad only had about a year to live, and I desperately wanted him to see me making a success of my life, yet I had over two years to go on my law degree. When I was offered a lucrative contract to play professional football, I thought, What the hell? It's only twelve months out of my life. Besides, it was money up front, money I could use to get some second opinions on Dad's cancer.'

'And?'

'Dad's health improved under new doctors, but by then I was trapped. The new treatments and medicines were expensive. One year became two, then three, then four. I became resigned to being a footballer forever and started thinking about my own financial future—in fact I'd just bought the penthouse—when Dad's health took a nosedive. Right about the same time, another new drug was discovered, one which promised a miracle cure. Which is why I did that rotten calendar. The drug didn't cure him, but it did seem to ease his pain, so it was worth it.'

'It must have been difficult for you, Roy, having to play football when you really didn't want to.'

'I can't say it was easy. But it was worth it to make Dad's last years happy ones. I think he was proud of me.'

'I'm sure he was,' she said, thinking to herself that he might not be so proud of his son now. Still, she could not deny that Roy had been a good son. Kind and thoughtful and, yes, noble in a way.

Thinking of Roy and nobility in the same breath irritated her. Noble men did not prostitute themselves, neither did they try to seduce women who didn't want to be seduced. At least . . . not unless the

seducer really cared about her. Kate plunged her hands
into the hot water and started attacking the plates.

'You know, Kate,' Roy interrupted after a minute
or two of noisy washing-up, 'I don't agree with your
assessment of your looks. You *are* pretty. And before
you jump down my throat I also agree I didn't see
you back then. But a lot of teenagers go through an
awkward physical stage. You should have seen me at
fifteen. I suddenly shot up without filling out. I was
all arms and legs. Couldn't get a girl to look at me if
I tried.'

Kate slanted him a sardonic look. 'I'll bet that
changed pretty quickly later on. I'll bet you were
fighting them off with broomsticks.'

'Hockey sticks, actually. At uni, the girls' hockey
team trained on the same field as the football team.
By then, I'd developed a few muscles.'

'And a reputation, no doubt,' was her dry
comment.

Her mother's appearance in the kitchen with the
last of the dirty utensils put paid to any more of that
conversation.

'Your father and I are going to bed now, Kate.
There are clean towels on your bed, Roy, and the
bathroom's right next to your room. Turn off the
lights, would you, Kate, before you go to bed?
Goodnight, then. See you in the morning.'

Kate's tension at suddenly finding herself alone with
Roy was instant and alarming. Still, she managed to
finish the washing-up very quickly, pulling out the
plug and drying her hands. But when she went to flee
the room, Roy's hand shot out to grab her arm.

'Don't go. I've been waiting all night to talk to
you alone.'

Her laugh was caustic. 'To get me alone, don't you mean? You just don't know when to give up, do you?'

Throwing the tea-towel down on the counter, he glared down at her. 'Oh, I think I do, Kate. I think I do.'

'Smart of you.'

His nostrils flared. 'One day, Kate Reynolds, you're going to get into trouble with that sharp tongue of yours.'

'And one day, Roy Fitzsimmons, you're going to get into trouble with that whole body of yours! Or haven't you thought of that?'

'I've been thinking about nothing else all weekend.'

'No kidding. As if I didn't know!'

'You know nothing about me, lady,' he lashed out. 'If you did, you'd never have jumped to the ridiculous conclusion about me you did. But there again, maybe that had more to do with *you* than *me*.'

Kate stared at him in shock and confusion. 'What . . . what are you talking about?'

'I'm talking about the fact that I am *not* a gigolo. Or an escort or a male prostitute or any damned thing like that! The only business Ned and I are in is a chain of gyms called The Body Beautiful.'

Kate was stunned. 'But . . . but . . . I heard you,' she argued shakily. 'On the phone that night . . .'

Roy raked both his hands through his thick black waves, his anger changing to exasperation. 'What you heard was my grumbling about the problems we were having with the various contracts we'd inherited from the previous operators. A lot of the women clients weren't happy with our new charges, not taking into account the amount of money we'd spent on doing up what were very run-down premises. Some of them were also complaining about the new timetable of aerobic and dancing classes, ignoring that we were now employing professional instructors instead of rank amateurs.'

Kate struggled to remember exactly what she had overheard, and it wasn't long before she realised that what Roy was saying fitted the scenario as easily—and a lot more acceptably—as the conclusion she'd come to. Though her embarrassment was acute, so was her fluster.

'Then why didn't you deny it?' she groaned. 'Why let me keep on thinking the worst?'

'Lots of reasons. I was furious with you for jumping to such a crazy conclusion at first. Didn't it ever occur to you that a high-profile person like myself could never make a go of such a scandalous profession? It would have been all over Sydney within no time!'

The thought had never occurred to Kate. To her, Roy had never been famous or high-profile, just a gorgeous young man who she was sure would never want her as she wanted him to. 'I . . . I . . . no, I didn't think of that,' she muttered wretchedly. 'I guess I just didn't think.'

'That was obvious! But the longer *I* thought about it, the more I realised I had to go along with the idea if I wanted to go on seeing you. At least for a while...'

'But that . . . that's *crazy*!'

'No, it's not. Once you told me what you thought I was, and jumped to the second conclusion about why I'd asked you out in the first place, I knew you wouldn't believe the truth. You were all for running away, Kate, because that was easier than facing facts that didn't fit your preconception of yourself—that I was actually attracted to you, that I found you interesting and intriguing, that I wanted to take you home to bed.'

'But you didn't!' she gasped. 'You couldn't! I mean . . .'

She broke off when she saw the look on his face.

'See? Even now, after all I've said and done, you can't accept the real reason why I'm here now. I want to be with you, Kate. I like you. I desire you.'

'But you can have any woman you want!' she wailed.

'That's very flattering of you to say so, but it's not true. For one thing, I want Kate Reynolds and I haven't done very well with her so far, have I?'

Kate was still rather bewildered. Why would a man like Roy want *her*? There had to be plenty of other women, far more beautiful and experienced, whom he could have pursued. Why chase after a thirty-year-old spinster whose sex-appeal rating was minimal and whose experience was zero? All she could think of was that maybe she'd somehow challenged his ego, or perhaps he fancied himself her first lover.

Whatever, it wasn't because he'd fallen madly in love with her. Men like Roy didn't fall madly in love with women like herself. Perhaps he was merely amusing himself with her. No doubt he'd had a good laugh at her expense, pretending he was for hire like that. More embarrassment flooded in, ingniting her quick temper.

'And you won't be doing any better now!' she pronounced with a flash of fire in her eyes. 'I haven't avoided men this long to have a one-night stand. I want more than that.'

His blue eyes darkened with an equal burst of fury. 'And you think I don't? Hell, Kate, if it was a one-night stand I was after, then what the heck am I doing here tonight? I could be back in Sydney, taking my pick of women!'

A flicker of hope fluttered in her heart, but she refused to let it take hold. 'Then why aren't you?' she flung at him. 'Why me, Roy? Tell me.'

His sigh was frustrated. 'If you have to ask that, then you're still running away from the truth. But you can't deny you want me, Kate Reynolds. You simply can't believe I could possibly want you back. You have to find a hook to hang my desire on to make it acceptable to your chronic inferiority complex. You've told yourself for so long that no man could want you that you really believe it. It's ingrained into your conscious mind.

'But your subconscious refused to listen the day you met me, my sweet. It responded to me on a purely primitive level, both in the park and in your office, that little tushy of yours wiggling its sexual message out loud and clear when you sashayed off to your washroom.'

Kate gasped. 'Don't be disgusting!'

'Sexual attraction isn't disgusting. It's perfectly normal. Which is why I asked you out. I wanted a woman that day. No, I *needed* a woman. Quite badly.'

'I find that very hard to believe.'

'Maybe so, but it's the truth all the same. I'd been working for months on refitting those gyms. Then our advertising agency decided I should be the star of our ad campaign. What a ghastly experience that was! Gruelling, in fact. I'd just finished on the last one the night before I met you. I remember getting home late that night and thinking I hadn't been with a woman in months. I fully intended seeking out some sexy young blonde to take to bed that weekend when I met you, and soon you were the only woman I wanted.'

Everything inside Kate felt as if it were going at a hundred miles an hour. Her hands came up to clasp her temples, trying to stop the blood from pounding in her veins. 'But I'm not blonde *or* sexy,' she moaned.

'Well, you're certainly not blonde,' he said. 'And I have met sexier women. On the surface. But you've made me want you more than I've ever wanted a woman before.'

His words took her breath away, suspending her heartbeat. 'I...I don't believe you,' she rasped, sucking in much needed air.

'I know.'

'You're...you're just saying that to get me into bed with you.'

'Do you honestly think I need lies to get you into bed with me, Kate?'

She simply stared at him.

'We both know I could get you into bed without such subterfuge. All I'd have to do is take you in my arms right now and start kissing you. You want to go to bed with me as much as I want to go to bed with you.'

His one-sided smile was slow and self-mocking. 'No...perhaps not that much. Because I'm simply dying to go to bed with you, Kate. I'm dying to strip all of those sexy clothes from your highly desirable body. I'm dying to do a hell of a lot of things, not the least of which is to just hold your naked, trembling flesh next to mine for hours on end...'

He wasn't even touching her, but the images his words evoked, the sensuality his eyes promised, propelled her into a state of instant sexual excitement.

She stared, wide-eyed, at him, a soft panting sound coming from her slightly parted lips.

'I can admit it, Kate,' he went on huskily. 'Can you? And if you can, when are you going to do something about it? Because the first move won't come from me, my love. It has to come from you.'

'Why?'

'You know why.'

'Do I?' She could hardly think, her eyes locked to his in an erotic trap that was sending her crazy.

'Think about it tonight when you're lying in that little-girl bed of yours. Then, when you're ready to be a woman again, let me know.'

With that, he turned and went to leave the room, stopping in the open doorway to throw one last glance back over at her. His eyes were hard and uncompromising, and for a second she almost hated him. For she knew he was right. She wanted him to make love to her very, very badly. She wanted him to do all those things he'd talked about. But most of all, she just wanted him.

'I'll be waiting,' was all he said.

CHAPTER TEN

KATE slipped into the guest room a little after three. She closed the door as quietly as her shaking hands would allow, then leant against it, certain that if the figure in the bed was asleep—as he seemed to be— then the sound of her heart banging away in her chest would waken him.

What on earth am I doing here? she agonised after a couple of excruciating seconds of standing there, shivering with fear and cold.

But she knew the answer.

It was lying over in that bed, sound asleep.

An angry frustration distracted her fear for a second. *She* hadn't been able to sleep. Not for a single second. Initially, she'd huddled on the side of her bed, listening to Roy showering. Then when doors opening and shutting indicated he had finally gone to bed she herself had gone into the bathroom and attempted to soothe her jangled nerves beneath hot jets of water.

It hadn't worked. If anything, it had made her worse, bringing her attention to wet naked flesh, making her want things she'd never wanted before. Desire, hot and strong, had raced through her veins, heating her brain as well as her body, sending her conscience flying in place of sizzling desires that would not be still, or stilled, no matter what she told herself.

Gradually, it didn't matter whether Roy was exaggerating his own feelings, or even lying. He did seem to want her. Maybe it was only because of severe frustration, or maybe she represented some sort of challenge to his male ego. Yes, that sounded right. There wouldn't be too many women who would have resisted him as she had done.

As for her own feelings . . . Kate was too inexperienced with men and relationships to be sure if what she felt for Roy was infatuation or a strong sexual attraction or something deeper. Whatever her feelings were, they were darned powerful, for here she was, prepared to do what Roy had challenged her to do—make the first move.

Yet the longer she stood with her back against that door, shivering in her pink satin nightshirt, the more her courage began failing her. Till at last it failed completely.

As powerful as her desire was, her fear of failure and ultimate rejection was greater. Whatever had possessed her to put herself on the line like that? She must have been totally insane! Perhaps she could slip out as unobtrusively as she had entered . . .

Her hand crept over to the knob. She started turning it.

'If you leave now,' a low male voice murmured from the bed, 'I won't ever speak to you again.'

Kate sucked in a ragged breath. 'I . . . I thought you were asleep,' she whispered shakily.

The figure moved, turning into the shaft of moonlight that slanted across the bed from the gauzily curtained window. Pushing back the quilt to display a disturbing amount of bare chest, he propped himself up on one elbow, then stretched over to pick up his wristwatch from the bedside table.

'Which would be highly likely at this hour,' he drawled after a glance at the time. 'But I'm a light sleeper. I take it you haven't come to have a heart-to-heart in the middle of the night?'

His sardonic tone fired a very welcome anger. 'You know damned well why I've come,' she spat.

'I hope so, Kate. I sincerely hope so.' He lifted the quilt in a gesture of invitation, the blatant showing of his nakedness under the bedclothes bringing an enormous lump to her throat.

Kate had wondered earlier, when she'd been lying alone in her room, whether Roy went to bed in the nude or not, the thought both tantalising and tormenting her. But the actual sight of his power-packed body lying there in the moonlight, every muscle beautifully defined, every startling and impressive inch on show, had a paralysing effect on her.

It seemed impossible that a person could be frozen, yet blistering hot, at the same time.

Yet Kate was. Literally. She stood there like a statue, staring at him, while inside a fire was stoking that was about to blow its stack.

'For pity's sake, woman,' Roy growled impatiently. 'Get yourself in here before I freeze to death.'

Gulping, she somehow propelled herself towards the bed, her steps gaining impetus with each stride. Finally, she practically dived under the covers beside him, aware of nothing but a mad pounding in her head and her heart. It was when he enfolded her hard against him that she began to shake uncontrollably.

'Hey,' Roy said as he rubbed her back and stroked her hair. 'What's all this about? You're not that cold, are you?'

'N-no,' she stammered, and shook all the more. 'I'm t-terrified.'

He held her close till her shaking quietened to the occasional quiver, then lay her gently back on the pillow and looked down at her still frightened face, an understanding light glowing in those beautiful blue eyes of his.

'There's nothing to be nervous about,' he soothed, smoothing her hair back from her face, then bending to kiss her lightly on the mouth. His smile was mischievous as his head lifted. 'We gigolos are experts at pleasing women.'

Kate felt her cheeks going red. 'Must you remind me of that?'

'Why not? It's rather flattering in a way.'

'I don't see how.'

'All those women I was supposed to be servicing at once. It's an awesome thought. Amusing too when you consider I hadn't been with even one woman in months.'

Kate wasn't sure if that fact pleased her or not. She didn't like to think frustration was the only reason he wanted her. 'I still find that hard to believe,' she muttered.

'Well, it's true. When you work as hard as I've been working, all you want to do when you get home at night is sleep. Do you realise I repainted the inside and outside of every one of those damned gyms all by myself? That was some job!'

'What about your partner, that Ned person? Doesn't he help at all?'

'I'm afraid Ned's not the best handyman in the world,' Roy said wryly, and Kate wondered if his partner was doing a bit of sponging. She suspected Roy might be a soft touch where his friends were concerned. Still, the man *had* lent Roy his car. That was a generous thing to do. Not many men would lend a mate their Mercedes Sports.

'You and Ned are good friends, aren't you?' she said softly.

'The best. We used to play football together.'

'Used to. Does that mean he's older than you, or did he retire injured as well?'

An odd cloud passed over Roy's eyes for a second, but then he smiled down at her. 'Hey, what is this? I thought you came in here for some action, not conversation, yet here you are, wanting to talk about other men. I'm the only man I want you concentrating on, Kate Reynolds. Now kiss me, woman, before I change my mind and throw you out of here.'

Kate was startled to find she'd been chatting away quite companionably in bed with a naked man. Her eyes flung wide with surprise just as Roy's descending face blotted out all view of his narrowed gaze. She barely had time to take a breath before those firm, sensual lips of his were covering hers and prying them open.

A whimpery sound forced its way from deep within her throat. Oh, God, would she never get used to the shock of his invading tongue, or the way her senses went wild as it slid into the moist depths of her mouth?

The kiss went on and on, till Roy rolled on top of her, and though he took most of his weight on his elbows she still gasped at the pressure of his huge frame enveloping her tiny one. With a groan he shifted slightly on to one elbow, pushing what felt like a knee between her legs, and spreading them wide, into which erotic gap he settled his muscular thighs with a relieved sigh.

'That's better,' he muttered thickly. 'Wouldn't want to squash my lovely little Kate.'

His lovely little Kate probably wouldn't have cared. There was a certain primitive pleasure in the feel of his body weight dominating hers like that, especially when it was naked. Dear heaven, but he was all hardness and strength and sheer male power. It made her feel so small and feminine and, yes, weakly submissive.

Yet along with the desire to be totally mastered by Roy's brute strength, Kate also felt a compulsive urge to touch him back, to explore those flexed muscles, to run her fingers down the taut lines of his body. She found herself doing so, thrilling to the way her caresses made him quiver convulsively. Having run her fingers down his sides and thighs, she moved to his back, splaying her hands wide and smoothing her palms down over skin like steel velvet. Her touch followed the dip of his waist, then rose to the swell of his buttocks. There she found herself gripping the softer, more malleable flesh, massaging it, kneading it, then, with a sudden surge of blind passion, grabbing him and pulling him closer into her.

His withdrawal was swift and abrupt, as he levered himself sharply upwards till he was sitting back on his heels between her thighs, the quilt like a huge tent over his shoulders.

'None of that, you little devil,' he warned with a wry laugh. 'I'm trying to make this good for you, and what do you do? Try to tempt me into a premature and—might I add—dangerous venture. Don't you know that's a sure way to get pregnant? Or worse?'

Kate stared up at him, face flushed, eyes wide with shock. How could she have forgotten, so soon after her own mother had warned her? What kind of nincompoop was she?

'Have . . . have you got something with you to use?' she asked shakily.

'Of course. That's rule number one in this world. Always carry protection with you if you aim to be sexually active.'

'And what's rule number two?'

'Never let sexy women start touching you before you're properly armed.'

'Ooh . . .' Her flush grew fiercer, though she was flattered that Roy thought her sexy. And she *did* feel sexy at that moment. Very sexy. It was all she could do to lie there without touching him some more.

'So!' he pronounced. 'We shall proceed according to Roy's rules. First, we will dispense with this nightwear. But no touching, now. You just lie still.'

Kate flinched when his hands went to the top button of the nightshirt, her stomach curling with a resurgence of that old inferiority complex. What if he didn't like her body? What if he preferred huge breasts, or a stomach like a washboard? What if she was too small all over, and in other places?

Her tension increased with each button.

He stopped at the last one, darting her a frowning look.

'What's up?' he asked intuitively.

'I . . . I guess I'm still a little nervous,' she admitted.

His smile was full of warmth and gentle understanding. 'I know, sweetheart. That's what I like best about you.'

'What . . . what do you mean?'

'The fact that I am the first man you've trusted like this in so long makes me feel really special, Kate. I'll

never betray that trust. It's all going to be good. More
than good. It's going to be the best. Now all I want
you to do is lie back and enjoy. It's your turn, Kate.
Your turn . . .'

My turn . . .

A soft moan escaped her lips when he drew the sides
of the satin shirt back, exposing her quivering flesh.

'Ah,' he growled, passing a deliciously tormenting
hand over her hard-tipped breasts. 'What an incredibly sexy little body you have.' And his head bent
to take one of those tips deep into his mouth.

Her gasp was involuntary and quite loud.

Roy stopped to frown down at her. 'I'm not hurting
you, am I?'

When she shook her head vigorously from side to
side he laughed softly and continued, alternating his
attentions from one breast to the other till she was
beside herself with she knew not what. Her arms lifted
to cover her eyes, for she no longer wanted to look
down at what he was doing. It was more than enough
to concentrate on the sensations rampaging through
her body, to try to stop herself from moaning and
groaning too loudly.

Yes, yes, do that one, she would groan silently to
herself when he left one aching tip to start on the
other, sighing her pleasure before moaning her frustration when the abandoned breast wanted the heat
of his mouth as well. Eventually, she didn't know what
she wanted. More, perhaps. But what?

When he started a slow, sensual journey down her
body, kissing and licking her as he went, she was past
caring. Everything was pleasure, making her head spin
and her body quiver.

But then she discovered that what she'd thought of as the ultimate in pleasure had been next to nothing, a mere bagatelle compared to the ecstasy she could experience under the expertise of Roy's lips and tongue.

'You mustn't,' she said at first when he scooped his hands up under her buttocks and lifted her melting flesh to his mouth. But it was a weak, unconvincing protest. For there was a magic in his mouth that Kate could not resist. She moaned softly under its sweet possession, dazzled by the sensations he could produce with those wonderful lips, those teasing teeth and that devouring tongue. Ah, yes, that darting, dancing, devouring tongue. How she craved its attention, even when it tormented her, flicking all too quickly over her sensitised flesh.

Kate was wallowing in Roy's highly intimate attentions when suddenly her breath caught, and a thousand stars burst within her head. A cry burst from her lips and her body arched upwards, squeezing tight before seemingly shattering into exquisite spasms of delight. When she finally sank back down into the bed, it was as though a wave were washing through her, bringing a sigh of utter contentment. But a degree of confusion as well.

She frowned up at Roy as he joined her, green eyes bewildered. When she opened her mouth to speak, he held a finger against her lips.

'Hush, now. This is just the beginning, not the end. Women are remarkable creatures, Kate. You can have many orgasms in one night, didn't you know that?'

She shook her head at him. She didn't know anything much about sex. Didn't he realise that?

'Best to continue, however,' he went on with a seductive smile, 'before you do something disastrous
like drift off to sleep. And I do something disastrous
like die of frustration.' Reaching across her body, he
picked up his wallet from beside his watch, extracting
a small plastic envelope then tossing the wallet away
on to the floor.

Kate watched, mesmerised, at the efficiency and
speed with which Roy drew on his protection.

'Stop staring at me like that, you bold minx. Surely
you've seen one of these before?'

She gulped, then blinked up at him. 'Not one quite
like that.'

'Are we still talking about condoms here?'

She shook her head and he chuckled. 'Is that a
compliment, or flattery?'

'A . . . a . . . fact.'

His laughter was highly amused. 'You sure are good
for my ego, Kate. So good that I think I might keep
you. Now come here,' he growled, and pulled her
under him. 'There's just so much noble sacrifice a
guy can take in one night. You've been driving me
mad, lover. Mad!'

Kate was totally distracted by the drowning intimacy of his kiss, so that when he eased himself between her thighs she was hardly aware of it. Even when
his hands roved down her back to clasp her buttocks,
she didn't realise he was positioning her for imminent
penetration. Her mind was focused on that passionate
tongue, working its will upon her senses, rousing her
again to fire and heat.

The alien and quite painful pressure of Roy's flesh
seeking entry into hers took her by surprise, making
her flinch and cry out.

With a gasp, he withdrew immediately, levering himself up on to his elbows. When he frowned down at her, blue eyes narrowed, Kate squirmed, her face turing aside from his scrutiny in anguished embarrassment.

I'm so stupid, she agonised. I must have hurt him in some way. Oh, God . . .

'You're a *virgin*,' he said, his tone full of shock.

Kate's head turned back, her expression blankly startled. Well, what had he thought she was? She'd told him she had no experience with men, hadn't she?

'Hell,' Roy muttered, and catapulted out of the bed, snatching up a robe that was draped over a chair. Turning away from her, he dragged it on before whirling back, his face not quite so stunned but still distressed. 'Why, in God's name, didn't you tell me?'

'I . . . I thought you knew.'

'How would I know? I naturally thought you'd slept with that bloke at university you told me about. Heck, you implied that you were once a little raver! I thought that was the problem when you overheard him saying what a sure thing you were. I presumed this was *after* the big event, since you were so traumatised by his comments. I never for one moment thought you'd never had sex before.'

'Does . . . does it make any difference?' she asked in a small voice.

Her insecure tone must have reached him, for he groaned, sat down beside her, and picked up her hand. 'Of course it makes a difference. If I'd known I'd have done things differently. I certainly wouldn't have . . .'

Kate was astonished to see him actually colour with embarrassment.

'Whatever must you have thought of me?'

'I thought you were rather wonderful,' she said with a catch of emotion in her voice. 'And I want you to finish what you started.'

He jumped up. 'Oh, no. No way.'

Tears pricked her eyes. 'You don't want me any more.'

'God!' He threw his hands up in exasperation. 'Of course I want you. Don't be ridiculous.'

She sat up and started doing the buttons of her nightshirt back up, a dark depression claiming her. 'It's all right. I . . . I understand. You don't want to be bothered with a virgin.'

Roy knelt down in front of her and clasped her hands tightly in his, but she refused to look at him, keeping her eyes steadfastly on the floor.

'You're wrong, Kate. Very, very wrong.'

'You shouldn't have stopped,' she choked out, tears threatening again.

'Darling Kate, do you honestly think you would have enjoyed it if I'd ignored your discomfort back then and simply ploughed on? Do you honestly think that at some point your pain would have turned to pleasure? That's rubbish. Romantic rubbish. For everyone that miracle happens to, there are hundreds who end up thinking sex is horrible. A good first experience requires a lot of patience and skill on the part of the man. I just wasn't prepared for it. But I will be next time.'

Her eyes snapped. 'Oh, really? And when, exactly, will the next time be? Or do I have to make the first move then as well?'

He smiled. 'You're angry with me.'

'Too right I am.'

'You shouldn't be. You had a lot more fun than I had.'

'Oh! Trust you to embarrass me by saying that.'

He drew her to her feet. 'When I've finished with you, Kate Reynolds, you won't find sex embarrassing on any level. Now get off to bed before I change my mind and do something I'll regret.'

'As if you could ever do anything *you'd* regret!' she threw at him as she tossed his hand away and flounced over to the door.

His low rumble of laughter followed her. '*You're* going to regret something pretty quickly if you keep up that noise. Or did you drug your parents' nightcaps in anticipation of this raucous little rendezvous?'

Kate froze, suddenly aware of how loudly she'd been talking. Thank heavens her parents' bedroom was at the other end of the hall.

'That's another reason I want to postpone this,' Roy said, coming forward to curl gentle hands over her shoulders. 'I don't want us having to whisper. I don't want there to be anything furtive when we finally make proper love. I promised you it would be the best, Kate. And the best is what I aim to deliver. Trust me . . .'

For a long, excruciating moment she stared up into his eyes, seeing their erotic promise, and finding it so exciting that she could feel the heat between her thighs.

'Kiss me goodnight,' she whispered, wanting one last feel of his arms around her.

'No,' Roy said abruptly, and stepped back from her. 'No more kisses. You've had more than your share tonight and I'd like some chance of getting a little sleep. God knows what both of us are going to look like in the morning . . .'

CHAPTER ELEVEN

THEY looked passable, Kate the better of the two. Roy definitely had dark rings under his eyes, but with his rugged looks that didn't look any worse on him than when he'd sported a three-day growth.

Kate found the whole day a trial, but she endured it without showing visible signs of frustration. Privately, it was a different story. She could not look at Roy without thinking of the night before, without reliving some of those incredible moments. Despite the unfortunate finale, the rest of Roy's lovemaking had been stunningly pleasurable. Yet he had implied better was still to come.

The weekend could not end quickly enough for Kate, despite its success where her family was concerned. The children adored Roy, especially when he played non-stop with them all afternoon. Her father sung his praises, as did everyone else.

Kate herself lapped up some considerable praise as well, everyone commenting on her appearance and her relaxed, happy manner, though most of the time this latter part was put on. Not that she wasn't happy. She was. Sort of. But she definitely wasn't relaxed.

Neither could she totally disregard a niggling worry over her new feelings for Roy. Before, she hadn't been sure exactly what she felt for him. Common sense demanded it couldn't be love, since she didn't know him well enough for that, and she did not believe in love at first sight. Lust at first sight she could accept. So she'd guessed her feelings were a combination of infatuation and lust. Not only was he gorgeous to look at—a heart-throb, her mother had called him—but he was different from any other man she'd ever met. He was cheeky and irreverent and amusing. Yet always he was a real man. Strong and decisive and, yes, very sexy.

It was this very sexy part, however, that was consuming her now, blotting out all else. Truly, she could not look at him without thinking about sex, without experiencing a tightening in her breasts and stomach.

And while she should have been relieved that she had finally become what Estelle would think of as 'normal', she was also somewhat disappointed in herself. She could have sworn only true love could have released these feelings in her, could have inspired such intense desires.

But true love seemed far from her mind all that day. Her thoughts were on nothing but how Roy had looked, lying there in the moonlight, and what had happened after she had joined him in that bed.

Kate slept badly that night and was quite relieved when they were on their way back to Sydney the following morning. She dragged in then exhaled a shuddering breath as soon as the Mercedes rounded the first corner.

'I'm glad that's over!' she exclaimed. 'Thanks for being such a good sport yesterday, Roy. It must have been a bit boring for you, playing games with the kids all afternoon.'

'I enjoyed it. I like kids.'

'And they liked you. The girls especially think you're the bee's knees. But then you were a big hit with all the females in the house, even Mum.'

'Oh, I wouldn't say that. I think I have a way to go before I gain Alice's complete approval. She doesn't entirely trust my intentions where her darling daughter is concerned.'

'Oh? What did she say?'

'Nothing too specific, but I was on the end of a few warning comments.'

'So was I.'

'Ah . . . the plot thickens. What did she say to you?'

'That if I had an affair with you, I should be careful.'

Roy's eyebrows shot up. 'Careful in what way?'

'You know . . . *Sexually* careful.' She slanted a slightly embarrassed look across at Roy. Oddly enough, he looked rather annoyed, frowning over at her.

'What in heaven's name did you say to your mother about me to make her think I would ever let anything like that happen to you?'

Kate was flustered by his unexpected anger. 'Nothing! I . . . I think she was worried about *my* doing something stupid. I guess she thought I might lose my head over you. She knows I've little experience with men.'

'A fact you seem keen to remedy,' he remarked drily.

His sarcasm sparked a sharp retort. 'And what's wrong with that? I thought you were all for my stopping running away from life and men. You should be proud that you've achieved the impossible—remade plain old Kate into a presentable-looking female, revved up her dead old engine, made her finally feel as if she wants to tear the clothes off a man!'

Roy's sideways glance carried a certain irony. 'How very complimentary! Is that all you want me for? Sex?'

'Are you saying you want more than that from me?' she countered archly.

'Perhaps,' he stunned Kate by replying.

Her eyes flung wide with shock. She hadn't accepted till that moment how much she wanted him to want more. Why, all that rubbish about her feelings only being lust was just that. Rubbish!

'But probably not,' he added drily.

Her dismay was so sharp that it infuriated her. Did she honestly think he'd been going to say he'd fallen madly in love with her? That he wanted to marry her, have babies with her? She could make herself over till the cows came home and she still wouldn't be the sort of woman Roy would eventually walk down the aisle with. Presuming he *wanted* to walk down an aisle with anyone. For all she knew, he might have already decided to opt for a swinging bachelor's life. A lot of men did these days.

Pride demanded she say something to stop his finding out the depths of her own emotional involvement.

'Let's not ever pretend this is anything more than it is, Roy,' she stated baldly.

'And what's that?'

'You're badly in need of a woman and I'm badly in need of a man.'

'Wow! That's brutally honest. I take my hat off to you. You've come a long way in one week. If that's the case, we might as well get down to the nitty-gritty. When is the big event to be? What about next Friday night? Or is that an inconvenient time?'

'What do you mean..."inconvenient"?' She frowned, disconcerted by his angry tone. She wondered why he was angry with her for calling a spade a spade. Did he like the women he bedded to declare undying love for him even if he didn't love them back? Did his male ego need that kind of stroking?

'Look, Kate, you're the one who doesn't want to be coy about this,' he went on, still brusquely. 'I promised you last night that the next time we were together it would be the best. I like to keep my promises. Tonight we'll both be tired after this trip. Tired does not make for good sex. The rest of this week is out as well, because *I'm* going to be flat out making up for being away three days. Ned and I are having a promotional cocktail party next Saturday night at our Paddington gym to launch our new advertising campaign, and I have heaps still to do. But by Friday I'll be in dire need of rest and recreation myself, so provided it's not the wrong time of the month...'

She tried hard not to cringe, both at Roy's blunt questioning and at his describing an evening with her as 'rest and recreation'. She'd asked for honesty and now she was getting it!

'No, it's not the wrong time of the month,' she muttered. 'That isn't till early next week.'

'Good. Friday night it will be, then.'

Both of them fell into a black silence, Roy putting his foot down, Kate sitting there in a wretched huddle. Her misery deepened with each passing mile, so when Roy's left hand suddenly settled on her thigh she was stunned. Her head jerked round to find him looking over at her with an apologetic smile on his face.

'I'm sorry,' he said. 'Forgive me?'

Kate's relief was enormous. She'd hated their arguing, hated Roy being angry with her.

'Of course.' She smiled back. 'Am I forgiven too?'

'No one should ever have to be forgiven for being honest. I'm acting like a fool, being touchy about something I've done myself a hundred times. I guess I didn't like the boot being on the other foot.'

Now his apology fell a little flat. So it *was* just his male ego sparking his anger. For a moment there she had hoped . . .

Kate gave herself a mental shrug. Don't go hoping for things that will never be, she told herself firmly. Just hold on to this moment. It's real. Roy's wanting you is real. Next Friday night will be real. If it was only going to be a sexual encounter on his part, then so be it. It was better than nothing.

'How about some music?' she suggested softly, and, removing his hand, switched on the radio. There was an Elvis love ballad playing, something about suspicious minds.

Kate settled back to enjoy the song, and the warm relief that had come with their making up. She tried hard not to think of futile hopes and dreams, looking instead for the good that might come of an affair with Roy. She would be less afraid of men in future, and more confident in herself as a woman. She might even eventually find someone else to love as much as she loved the man sitting next to her.

Kate clung to that hope, for if she didn't she knew she would cry.

'I've brought something in for you,' Estelle said within seconds of her arriving at work the following morning.

Kate glanced up from where she was already sitting at her computer, pretending to be studying yesterday's foreign-market fluctuations. 'Oh? What?'

'Da-dah!' the girl exclaimed, unfolding a rather rumpled poster with a flourish.

Kate's mouth dropped open. For there, before her eyes, in all his glory, was the hunk of the month for January of the previous year. Only the towel he was holding stopped the picture from being a full-frontal nude.

'So!' Estelle was grinning. 'Is this to take pride of place in your bedroom, or shall we use it as a dartboard?'

Kate swallowed convulsively as she continued to stare at the poster. She'd known he was beautiful, but this wasn't just beauty. This was male perfection.

'Boss?' Estelle prodded, dropping one corner of the poster to wave a hand in front of Kate's face. 'Are you still here?'

Kate gathered herself quickly, a self-mocking smile curving her mouth. 'I think you'd better put something as distracting as that in a dim, dark filing cabinet, don't you?'

'You've got to be joking! That would be sacrilege. Well, if you don't want it I'll just have to pin it up in the tearoom. The other girls will——'

Kate leant over and snatched it away, dumping it down on her desk. 'Oh, no, you won't, missie. Not if you want to go on working for me.'

Estelle grinned. 'Whatever you say, boss. So how is it going with our esteemed sportsman? Did you take him home with you on the weekend?'

'Of course not,' Kate denied brusquely, and swung to the computer screen once more.

'That's a relief.'

Kate's eyes snapped round and up. 'What do you mean by that?'

'A footballer friend of mine who once knew Roy said he's an incorrigible womaniser. Sweeps girls off their feet, then into bed, then dumps them. They never last for more than a week. You wouldn't want to take him too seriously, Kate. Men like that never change their spots.'

Kate stared down at the poster of Roy, seeing his extraordinary sex appeal, and knowing that what Estelle was saying was probably true. There'd undoubtedly been many women in his life. He'd admitted as much. And yet as she stared down into those beautiful blue eyes, she saw a vulnerability there that questioned his reputation as a callous womaniser. Maybe Roy just hadn't met the right woman yet, one who would love him with all her heart, one who would make him want more than a succession of one-night stands.

'You aren't going out with him again, are you?' Estelle asked with worry in her voice.

'Maybe,' she said, not wanting to tell any more lies. 'But don't worry, I won't take him seriously. Now, how about getting us both some coffee? I've a lot of work to catch up on and I need sustenance.'

As soon as Estelle left, Kate gave the poster one last long, lingering look before folding it up very carefully and depositing it in a drawer she rarely used. Some day, she vowed, brushing away a couple of rogue tears, some day she might have the courage to take that poster out and look at it again.

But that would not be for a long time to come, she believed, long after the real thing was nothing but a

dim memory in her heart. For she just could not believe that she would be that special woman to capture
Roy's heart. That was a pipe-dream. Better to grab
what small part of his life he was offering. It might
only be a night, or a week, or maybe two. Whatever,
she refused to start pining for more. To do so was the
road to despair.

Friday dawned overcast, but by the afternoon it had
warmed to a pleasant autumn day.

Roy had telephoned her the previous evening at
home, checking the arrangements for Friday night.
Kate was surprised, and somewhat hurt, by the cool
brevity of the call. Was his boredom with her already
setting in? she'd wondered wretchedly.

Now that D-Day had dawned, however, she found
it hard to remain totally depressed. A simmering excitement took hold during the course of the morning,
turning her mind to more positive thoughts. Tonight
Roy would take her in his arms again, kiss her again.
Tonight he would make love to her for real.

Kate left work at five-thirty, walking the short distance from her office to Roy's apartment block in a
few minutes. He'd offered to pick her up personally
but she'd refused, saying she preferred it this way.

Nerves crowded in as she pushed through the glass
doors and walked over to the security desk, though
she did her best to look as coolly composed as she
imagined a sophisticated career woman would look
on her way to an assignation with her lover.

Once passed by Security, she made her way to the
lifts and pushed the button. A man in a sleek business
suit, and carrying a briefcase not dissimilar to her
own, was also standing there. As they waited, he eyed

her up and down, his expression both curious and assessing.

Does he know why I'm here? she wondered shakily. Has he guessed? What is he thinking? Probably that I'm not dressed for a romantic rendezvous in this plain grey suit. Or is he speculating that it's hiding sexy black underwear?

It wasn't.

Kate had considered dressing differently from her usual office garb, but a weird type of rebellion had stopped her from doing another make-over on herself. Aside from applying a small amount of make-up and perfume, she was very much the same Kate that Roy had first seen that day in the park.

And why not? She was not and never would be a woman given to vampish tricks or exotic underwear. Oh, it had been fun at the weekend to shock her family into seeing that she *could* be different, but it wasn't really her, especially not in public. So it seemed likely, she decided, that the man beside her was not having any sexual thoughts about her at all. It was her own guilty imagination.

By the time Kate was knocking on the penthouse door, her nervous excitement was being tinged with worry. How would Roy react to her appearance?

The door was wrenched open and that knowing blue gaze swept over her. 'It doesn't take you long to slip back into old habits, does it, Kate?' he drawled, a drily sardonic edge in his voice.

'Nor you,' she returned tartly. 'Or do you always meet a girl at the door wearing nothing but a bathrobe?'

Anger blazed in his eyes for a split second before he casually opened the dark blue robe to show that he was wearing a pair of brief black swimming-trunks. 'I was filling in time till you came, doing a few laps. Swimming defuses tension. You should try it some time.'

'Perhaps I will,' she said, squeezing her eyes briefly shut as she turned to place her briefcase down beside the door.

The evening had certainly not begun well. When she had first seen his reproachful face Kate's old lack of self-confidence had raised its ugly head again, but, in contrast to the past, this time it had fired a surge of temper within her, resulting in her intial cutting retort.

But that flash of fire had died with his showing her his magnificent body like that, replaced by a sagging feeling of inadequacy. She should have realised this could happen, that her courage would fail her, that she would somehow revert to that old frightened Kate.

When she straightened and turned to face him once more, Kate was astonished to find Roy staring at her with the strangest look. It was oddly pained. But then he sighed and shrugged. 'I suppose this is nothing more than I deserve after the way I've treated women all these years,' he muttered, 'to have someone like you come along. But damn it all, Kate, you could have at least taken some trouble with yourself today.'

'Why?' she returned a touch bitterly. 'This is the real me. Don't you want the real me?'

'I could say the same to you, Kate. Do you want the real me? You're not the first woman who's wanted to tear my clothes off, you know. But it's not the real me they wanted, only the image, the football hero, the legendary stud.'

'I didn't know you were any of those things when I first met you,' she defended unhappily.

'But you know now, don't you?'

'I've heard stories . . .'

'Before or after you hired me for the weekend?'

She blushed furiously. 'You know that's not how it was, Roy. You're twisting things.'

'Do I?' His laughter was dry. 'Well, maybe I do, but it's all boiled down to the same thing in the end. Still, who am I to disappoint your expectations? Come . . .' And, taking her hand, he began drawing her up the winding staircase on her right.

For the briefest of moments she resisted, but when he directed a mocking glance over his shoulder she sighed her surrender. For he was right, wasn't he? To resist now would be hypocrisy at its highest. She'd come ostensibly to enjoy his body, not his person. She'd stripped this encounter down to its most basic level because, in her heart of hearts, she believed sex was all Roy was looking for with her anyway. He'd admitted it to her once. He'd wanted a woman. Badly. That was why he'd asked her out in the first place.

OK, so somewhere along the line his lust had become entwined with some degree of curiosity and interest in her. And his ego was bruised that a woman would dare do to him what he'd done to them for years. But he was very right when he said it would all boil down to the same thing. He would take her to bed, possibly enjoy himself with her for a while, but eventually he would grow bored and discard her. This way, she was making sure he knew *she* knew the final outcome. Their inevitable parting would not hurt as much if she didn't start wanting and hoping for more.

'If I'm to fulfil all your fantasies, Kate,' he drawled on the way up that elegant black staircase, 'then you must promise to do as I say. No more pulling back. No silly reticence.'

Kate gulped. Surely he wouldn't ask her to do anything . . . peculiar . . . would he?

No, no, her knowledge of him soothed. He was very much a normal man with normal desires. He was not a pervert or a sadist. He was, however, a very passionate and uninhibited individual, she accepted, a wave of dizzying weakness washing through her as she thought of what lay ahead.

'Kate?' He tugged at her hand.

She glanced up, realising she had stopped again. 'I'm coming,' she said, and scuttled up those last steps only to grind to a startled halt when she reached the top. For there, before her eyes, stretched an indoor swimming-pool of such enormous size and wicked opulence that she could do nothing but gape. When Roy had spoken earlier of doing a few laps, she'd imagined he'd used a communal pool, on the roof, perhaps. But this . . . this was extraordinary.

Never had she seen such a pool, except perhaps in books on the lavish decadence of the early Roman empire. The exquisite tiling on the sides drew her eyes, intricate mosaics in various shades of blue depicting exotic-looking fish seemingly leaping out of the water. The floor of the pool was blue as well, giving it a deep aqua colour. At the moment, the water lay icily still, like a sheet of blue glass, not a ripple on its surface.

Yet Kate could well imagine nubile young slave girls draped along the smooth ledges that lined the pool, trailing languorous hands in the water. They would be scantily clad, of course. If they were clad at all.

Maybe they would be nude, lying there casually dropping grapes into the mouths of their masters as they floated idly on the surface of the cool, pristine water.

Finally, Kate dragged her eyes past the pool to where she was equally startled to see a table and two chairs sitting in front of a huge picture window. For there was nothing remotely decadent in this intimate dining area. It was sheer romance—a candlelit setting for two, complete with white linen tablecloth, crystal glasses and champagne on ice. There was even a single red rose in a slender glass vase.

She walked past the pool to stare up close, first at the table again, then at the view. Dusk had just come upon the city and the lights had begun winking on. It looked glorious.

'Like it?' Roy asked softly from just behind her.

She turned to him, still stunned, and quite touched. He must like her a lot to go to so much trouble. Or was this his usual seduction scenario? 'It's very...romantic-looking,' she said, frowning at this last thought.

He laughed. 'And there I was, thinking you might like some romancing. More fool me!'

'But I do!' she insisted, surprised at how super-sensitive he was.

'If you say so,' he tossed off with cold indifference. 'The in-house catering service will deliver our meal in another hour or so. Meanwhile, I thought you might like to relax in the pool. And before you say you don't have a swimming-costume, I don't want you to use one,' he said harshly. 'Now let me show you where the bathroom is. You can leave your clothes in there.

You'll also find a spare robe hanging up behind the door. Feel free to use that if you want to.'

If she wanted to? The man had to be mad if he thought she was going to prance around in the nude. She was a long way off being one of those imaginary slave girls. And what about when the delivery person arrived with their meal? Bad enough that they would be lounging around in bathrobes. She shuddered. God, she wasn't cut out for this kind of *dolce vita* lifestyle. She was far too inhibited.

'Roy, I—er—I—um . . .'

Her voice died with his steely glance.

'L-lead on,' she said weakly.

'That's more like it.'

She showered after undressing and before putting on the thick red robe. Not especially because of hygiene, but as a delaying tactic. But the moment came when she could not delay her emergence any longer. When she did come out, Roy was sitting idly on one of the ledges beside the pool, swinging his feet in the water. His robe was nowhere in sight, but at least he had on a costume, whereas she would be defenceless against his all-seeing gaze if she took hers off.

'Ah, so there you are. I thought you might have melted and gone down the drain.'

No such luck . . .

'Hop straight in,' he drawled. 'It's heated.'

She was on the opposite side of the pool to him, a good twenty feet away. But it felt like twenty inches. The urge to run away was strong, but when she saw him looking at her in a challenging fashion her pride would not allow it. Lifting her chin, she held his eyes while she unsashed the robe and dropped it to the tiles, before diving fairly gracefully into the water.

When she surfaced to slick a few stray strands back from her face it was to find Roy clapping a slow clap.

'Bravo! For a while there I was sure you were going to bolt.'

Sarcasm had always spurred her to retaliate in kind, and now was no different. 'And abandon the experience of a lifetime? Come, now, Roy, do I look a fool?'

Her counter-attack sent a blaze of fire into those beautiful blue eyes of his. Deliberately but angrily, he stood up and stripped the already brief costume from his flesh, flinging it away just before he too dived into the pool. Now Kate turned to flee, but he was too fast, too strong, coming up to grab her forcibly by the shoulders and spinning her to face him.

'Yes,' he ground out. 'You're a fool. You could have far more than you're asking, Kate Reynolds. But this is what you've settled for and by hell I'm going to enjoy giving it to you.' And cupping one large hand around her chin, he grabbed her hair-knot with the other, holding her solidly captive while his mouth bent to hers.

Amazingly, despite his obvious anger, his kiss was not savage. It was, however, extremely thorough, demanding a response and getting it. Not that Kate had ever had any resistance to his kisses. In no time her arms had wound up around his neck and she was kissing him back with all the ardour and pent-up emotion within her sex-starved body.

He groaned, his hands dropping to enfold her breathtakingly close, one splayed across the middle of her back, the other sweeping down to curve round her buttocks. As he lifted her, her legs floated apart then found a natural and comfortable home wrapped around his waist. When moist lips started trailing down her throat, she automatically arched her back, offering her breasts up to the magic of his mouth.

He didn't disappoint her, and soon she was exulting in his expert attentions, closing her eyes and letting the exquisite feelings pulsate through her. The pleasure was all-consuming, leaving no room for thought or doubts or fears. She was all woman beneath Roy's hands and lips, wanting nothing but his kisses and caresses. Dazedly, she felt his fingers in her hair, extracting the pins, so that soon her curls were being unravelled on the surface of the water, spreading out in an erotic circle around her head. His hands moved down into the middle of her back, lifting her slightly from the water so that he could take more of her breast into his mouth. She moaned softly, never wanting him to stop.

Till suddenly she felt his arousal jabbing up between her buttocks. As swift as lightning, her focus shifted, her dazed pleasure abruptly turning to a knife-twisting frustration. The desire to be filled, to have him push deep and hard into her, was intense.

She groaned, and, gripping his shoulders, pulled herself upwards, her wet hair falling into a sodden curtain down her back. The new position changed the angle of her body, and as her hips began to rock backwards and forwards the hard tip of his erection rubbed across the hot, wet valley of her very aroused flesh.

'No,' he growled. 'Don't do that.'

'But I want to!' she gasped.

'No, Kate. Not yet. It's too soon.'

'No, it's not,' she cried in anguished desperation. 'It's not.' And she started covering his neck with

savage little kisses, suckling at his flesh, nipping at
the skin with a wild, wanton abandon. Her arms swept
down under his arms and around his back, her nails
digging into his shoulder-blades, her hips undulating
against him with a raw, naked need.

'Hell, Kate...'

But any resistance in Roy was short-lived. He
groaned his own frustration before abruptly and devastatingly doing what she was inviting, what she
craved.

His penetration brought both their heads up with
startled cries.

'You're so tight,' he said thickly. 'So damned tight.
I didn't hurt you, did I?'

She shook her head. 'No. It...it feels...fantastic.'

His smile was rueful. 'I'll second that.'

'What now?' she whispered.

'Give me a moment to catch my breath, you little
wildcat.'

'Oh.' Memory of her frantic actions sent a flush of
embarrassed colour into her cheeks and she buried
her face in his neck, ashamed now to meet his knowing
eyes. Perhaps Trevor was right about me, she conceded, but without too much distress this time. For
she rather liked her capacity to feel such intense
passion. She certainly liked what she was feeling at
that moment.

'Make love to me, Roy,' she whispered, kissing his
neck again, more softly this time and infinitely more
seductively.

'I intend to,' he said. 'But it will be better—and
safer—if we get out of the pool and head for my
bedroom.' And he started wading through the water
towards the shallow end.

Kate's face flamed some more as she realised what he meant by safer. Dear lord, her mother had been right to worry about her where Roy was concerned. Whenever he came near her, it was a case of off went her head and on went a pumpkin. Still, his responsible and caring nature only increased the love she felt for him, and her arms tightened around his neck.

'Why is it better out of the water?' she whispered.

'Water dulls the senses.'

'Really?' If what she was feeling at the moment was dulled, then heaven only knew what was awaiting her.

He reached the steps and slowly, carefully, emerged from the pool, carrying her with him. Immediately she knew what he meant. With the water left behind, she was much more fiercely aware of their bodies locked tightly together and the electric sensations caused by even the slightest movement.

Yet her pleasure was more than sexual. There was something incredibly moving about being joined this way with the man she loved. It was the ultimate intimacy, the ultimate trusting. And she did trust Roy. Completely. He'd just shown her how trustworthy he was, how worthy of being loved.

There was a welling of emotion in her chest and she closed her eyes, pressing passionate lips against his throat.

Roy's kicking a door open snapped her head up and her eyes open. They were in a bedroom dominated by a huge raised water-bed, which was dimly lit by recessed lights set into the ceiling above. The carpet looked cream, the walls pale blue, the bed royal. The wardrobes along one whole wall had mirrored doors which danced back erotic images of their entwined nudity.

Kate gasped when Roy sat down on the end corner of the bed, the undulation of the water-filled mattress bringing the most incredible feelings. Roy must have thought so too because he gave a muffled moan, closing his eyes tightly and taking a deep breath.

'Don't . . . don't you have to attend to something?' she asked tremulously after a few seconds.

His eyes half opened and he smiled an incredibly sexy smile. 'All in good time, lover. All in good time.'

His mouth bent to her lips, sipping at them softly for a while as he played with her breasts, the kiss growing hungrier as her nipples hardened to rock-like pebbles under his teasing fingers. Only when she began to make whimpering sounds did his hands slide down her sides to splay wide around her hips. Gripping her firmly, he then began moving her body in the most exciting fashion, sliding her back and forth across his water-slicked thighs. She didn't even try to still her soft moans of pleasure, though she groaned with dismay when he stopped and lifted her from him.

Till she remembered why he had to stop. Then she smiled at him with gratitude and love. He was remarkably quick, returning rapidly to lie her down on the satin quilt and gather her close, kissing her once more before gently and carefully entering her again. Her breathing was coming fast in her ears now, a wild heat racing through her veins. Quite instinctively, her legs moved to wrap tightly around him, her own body urging him into a vigorous and incredibly exciting rhythm.

When it came, Kate's climax far surpassed what she'd felt that night under Roy's lips, both physically and emotionally. As soon as her body started contracting around his, her heart filled with a sense of joyful loving so acute and intense that tears flooded her eyes. She thrilled to the sensations of her body, especially when *her* pleasure quickly became *his* pleasure, his body spasming into her within seconds. His arms tightened around her at that moment, and when he gasped her name Kate knew she would never feel as overwhelmingly happy as she did at that moment, nor as complete. This was her first man, her first act of love. And she loved him with all her heart.

CHAPTER TWELVE

THE evening was magic. Pure magic.

The candlelit meal; the champagne; the love-making. Kate felt as if she'd been swept into another world where fantasies did come true and reality was at least twenty floors away.

As midnight crept round she was standing with Roy on his private balcony, sipping the last of the champagne, staring down at the view, feeling as giddy with happiness as only a woman who'd just been beautifully made love to for an exquisitely long time could feel.

'I don't want this evening to ever end,' she whispered.

Roy's arm stole around her waist and she laid her head against him.

'Stay the night,' he suggested.

She flicked thoughtful eyes up at him. He looked tired. 'No, Roy. You need your sleep. You've got a busy day tomorrow.'

'Today, don't you mean?' Taking her near-empty glass, he placed it on the ledge and turned her in his arms. 'Promise you'll come with me to the party tonight. You said you would earlier.'

Her laughter was soft. 'I would have promised you anything at that moment.'

Kate was taken aback to see her comment annoyed him. He yanked her hard against him, and astonishingly she could feel through their robes that he wanted her again. 'Would you, indeed?' he growled. 'Well, maybe I could force a few more promises with a little further persuasion.'

His hands were quite savage, dragging the robe apart and down off her shoulders, baring her breasts to the cool night breeze and his hot mouth. Kate was initially shocked by the roughness of his attentions, though she soon found herself getting excited. But when she arched her back in response, her head tipping back, her loose hair knocked the glass from the ledge. Crying out, she tried to twist out of Roy's iron grasp, but he would have none of it, sweeping her up into his arms and carrying her back inside the dimly lit bedroom.

'You'll break more than a glass before you're finished, Kate Reynolds,' he snarled, and, dumping her on the water-bed, he stripped off his robe. She stared up at him, her heart thudding, aware of little but his huge dark shape as it loomed over her. Suddenly she was afraid.

'You . . . you wouldn't hurt me, would you, Roy?' she asked shakily.

His laughter was harshly dry. 'Hurt you? I'd like to strangle you. But no, Kate,' he rasped, his hands untying her robe and spreading it wide on the bed. 'I won't hurt you.' And with a groan he joined her on the bed and started making love to her yet again.

Kate was not a stupid woman. Somewhere during that long, tormented mating she realised Roy was angered by the fact she seemed to be using him just for sex. Was it still only a bruised male ego? she wondered dazedly. Or did he really want her to care for him?

After the storm had subsided, and Roy lay spread-eagled and exhausted across her, Kate began idly stroking his back. With an instinctive sensuality that she was only beginning to explore, she lifted her foot and caressed the hard planes of thighs, moving up over the softer flesh of his buttocks. God, but she loved the feel of his body. She settled her big toe into the crease of his buttocks and began to slide it up and down.

Roy shuddered, and rolled abruptly from her with a grimace on his face. 'Good grief, Kate, are you trying to kill me?'

'I could have said the same of you earlier.'

His face actually darkened with a guilty flush. 'Yeah, well, I guess I was a little rough. Sorry.'

'Don't be. I rather liked it.'

He glared over at her.

Rolling over on top of him, she kissed him softly on the mouth. 'I think you're the greatest lover in the world.'

'Gee, thanks,' he muttered testily. 'Just what I always wanted to hear.'

'Most men would.'

'Perhaps I'm all complimented-out these days. Perhaps I'm fed up with women seeing me as little more than a piece of meat.'

Kate stared down at him, appalled that he would think that was how she viewed him. She thought him a wonderful man, kind and gentle in some ways, but strong and masterful when he needed to be. Suddenly, to keep her true feelings hidden from him seemed not only wrong but cruel and destructive.

'Maybe I have something else to say that you might prefer hearing,' she said, nerves making her voice shake.

Roy eyed her warily.

She reached up to lay a tender, trembling hand against his cheek. It felt rough beneath the softness of her palm. 'I . . . I love you, Roy.'

She felt him flinch beneath her words, and while she waited anxiously for him to answer her, to say anything, he simply covered her hand with his and sighed.

'You . . . you don't *believe* me?' she gasped, and sat up, snatching her hand away.

He looked uncomfortable. 'Kate . . . it's a common enough mistake, confusing sex and love. Very common, if the person hasn't had much experience, be it either man or woman.'

'But . . . but I do! I've loved you all along, from that very first day!'

'Kate,' he said with a weary patience. 'That was merely sexual attraction. I felt it. You were attracted to me. You did not fall in love with me.'

'Well, maybe,' she conceded, 'but . . . but I love you now.'

'If you say so.' His wry smile was almost patronising, and it infuriated her.

'I do say so,' she insisted. 'But I won't be saying it again, believe me.'

'Good.'

'Good?' she exploded.

'Yes, good,' Roy stated sternly. 'Now lie back down and go to sleep. It's after two and we're going to be wrecks tomorrow if we don't.'

Feeling too tired to flounce out of the room and go home, Kate flopped back down on the bed, stiffening when Roy put his arms around her. But eventually, sheer exhaustion won the day and she fell asleep. It was the man who was cradling her against him who found it hard to drift off. He kept on thinking about the woman in his arms and her disturbing declaration.

If only it were true, he thought bleakly. But he doubted it. He'd been there, done that once. Which was why he could now recognise the difference between lust and love. A person often *thought* he or she loved their first lover. But they usually didn't . . .

Kate did not linger in the morning. She found waking naked in Roy's bed an awkward and embarrassing experience, and, quite frankly, she could not get out of there fast enough. He didn't believe she loved him. He thought her naïve and silly. She felt a complete fool.

Roy called her a taxi and took her down personally, but she had trouble meeting his eyes as he said his goodbyes. 'I still want you to come tonight,' he insisted. 'I'll pick you up at seven.'

She couldn't bring herself to say no, which had the awful effect of making her almost agree with Roy's assessment of her feelings for him. Maybe she didn't love him. Maybe it *was* only a sex thing, for she could not deny that one of the reasons she was agreeing to go to his party was because she hoped the evening would end in his bed again. Was that love? Or just lust?

By the time Kate let herself into her flat she was more confused than ever.

'What do you say, Pippa?' she asked the little yellow canary as she topped up her food and water. 'Do I love the man or not?'

Pippa gave a small whistle.

'Was that a yes? In that case I agree with you. But Roy doesn't. He thinks it's just lust.'

Kate sighed and flopped down on a kitchen stool, a new line of thought bringing more confusion. Since Roy didn't seem to want her love, why had he been so angry when he'd thought she was using him just for sex? Ego again? Or could there be some other explanation?

Kate shot to her feet as an idea struck, her heart racing madly. Could it be that he *was* beginning to fall in love with her? Could the miracle have happened that *she* was the one special woman so far in his life who could capture his heart? If that was so, then he would be rightly annoyed at being used as a sex object, but also wary of believing her when she'd seemed to do an about-face by saying she loved him.

Kate herself grew instantly wary of this new concept. It sounded too good to be true, but once the idea took hold she could not totally dismiss it. It *was* possible, wasn't it? Roy was capable of love. She was sure of it.

Whatever, it made her do everything she could to please him when it came to her appearance that night. She wore the leather outfit he'd chosen, left her hair out, and put on plenty of make-up and perfume. But it was all worth it when she saw the look of pleasure on Roy's face. His gaze swept down then up her body, a warm admiration lighting his eyes.

His own appearance was worth waiting for as well, his elegantly tailored grey trousers topped by a finely striped blue and grey shirt then completed with a dark blue blazer-style jacket. Freshly shaven, and with his wavy black hair slicked back from his strongly featured face, he looked very suave and handsome. And she told him so.

His smile seemed one of genuine satisfaction. 'I thought it was the man's job to compliment the woman.'

Kate shrugged. 'I guess I'm not up on that kind of thing. This is only the second real date I've had with a man.'

It was the wrong thing to say.

'Ah, yes,' Roy said drily. 'So it is.'

Unhappy with herself, Kate spun away to pick up her keys and bag, turning back with a stiff smile on her face. 'Shall we go?'

'By all means.'

'I see Ned lent you his car again,' she said when he led her over to the Mercedes.

'Not really. I bought it from him. He didn't need it any more.'

'Oh? Why's that?'

'Ned can't drive a normal car these days. He's a paraplegic.'

Kate's eyes widened before she groaned in sympathy for the poor man. 'Oh, how sad. How did it happen?'

'On the football field a few years back. And you'd better hide that pity around him or you'll find you have a tiger by the tail. Ned's not into pity.' He opened the passenger door and waved Kate into the car.

Is any of us? Kate mused on the slow drive over the bridge. Now another concept filtered into her mind. How much pity had there been in Roy's initial asking her out? Was it pity, perhaps, that had inspired him to go home to Armidale with her, and which had propelled him to take her to bed? It seemed Roy was a good Samaritan at heart, a lover of underdogs. Why else take on a paraplegic as a business partner in a physical-fitness venture? It seemed an odd choice.

A lover of underdogs...

Was that what she was to him? An underdog? Was it his plan to patch up all those old wounds and insecurities of hers, then send her on her way, all prettied-up and confident with the opposite sex?

Kate was horrified when all of a sudden tears welled up in her eyes. She'd much prefered her other idea, the one where Roy was madly in love with her.

Blinking furiously, she turned to watch the other cars inching their way into the city, forcing herself to focus on them, to think of anything else but her growing despair.

Saturday night was a big night in Sydney. The traffic was heavy and tediously slow, but within each vehicle sat people probably filled with anticipation and excitement, fired by Saturday night fever. There were dinners waiting to be eaten, movies and plays to be seen, discos to be danced at. Lovers would walk hand in hand around the harbour's edge, looking into each other's eyes, uncaring of anything but just being with each other.

Oh, God, she thought, and blinked some more.

'I'd better warn you,' Roy said abruptly. 'There'll be some members of the media at this party. We'll also be showing those ads we've made starring yours truly.'

'Doing what, Roy?'

'Just about everything physical you can think of short of you know what. Not that that wasn't suggested as well. The advertising people we're using seem to think sex sells everything.'

Kate thought of the poster she had in her desk drawer and realised any ad with Roy in it would be a huge success. 'Are you wearing clothes this time?' she asked, and slanted him a wry grin.

'Too damned right I am.'

'Not many, I'll warrant.'

'Enough. Brother, will we never get off this damned bridge?'

'I should have taken a taxi to your place.'

'Too late now. Ah, well...' He shrugged resignedly. 'I dare say Ned can hold the fort till I get there. No use in worrying about things you can't change.'

'No,' Kate murmured, thinking to herself that was another good philosophy. She couldn't *make* Roy love her. All she could do was enjoy the times he spent with her and make them as pleasurable as possible so that he kept coming back for more. 'Oh, look, that's why we've been so long; a car's broken down and we're having to merge into one lane. Once we get past the trouble-spot, it'll be all smooth sailing.'

It was, and in five minutes they were in Paddington and pulling into the car park of a rather gaudily painted warehouse-style building. Most of the façade was basic grey but with pink and mauve stripes diagonally across corners and a neon-lit sign which shouted THE BODY BEAUTIFUL in bold flashing letters.

'You can close your mouth now, Kate,' Roy said drily as he switched off the engine.

'Yes, well, it's—er...'

'Visible,' he finished crisply.

'True.'

'It'll attract clients.'

'I have no doubt.' So will your ads if you've done them in pink and mauve tights...

Her face must have reflected her cheeky thoughts.

'If you laugh once tonight, Kate, I'll make you pay.'

A giggle escaped. 'How?'

'I'll think of something,' he said darkly, and, taking her arm, guided her quickly up the stairs, through the pink and purple front doors and into a surprisingly classy grey and white foyer, filled with people drinking and talking. Some aerobic-style music thumped away in the background.

'So there you are!' a voice boomed, and a barrel-chested man in a wheelchair manoeuvred himself through the throng, coming up to them with a wide smile on his very good-looking face. 'And this must be Kate.'

When he held out his hand she gave him hers. But he didn't shake it; instead he used his not inconsiderable strength to pull her down so that he could kiss her on the cheek. 'Never let a chance go by to kiss a beautiful woman,' he said with a jolly laugh.

Despite his good cheer, Kate felt real pity for Ned flooding in. He was such a handsome man, and no more than thirty. But when a lovely-looking young woman walked up behind him, smiling as she curved loving hands over his shoulders, Kate's pity changed to curiosity.

'Are you flirting again, Ned?' the attractive brunette reproached softly. 'Hi, Roy. Is this your Kate? Hi, Kate. I'm Marla, Ned's wife.'

Kate was bowled over by Marla's beauty and charm. It quickly became clear that she was very devoted to Ned, who was an amazing man, full of drive and spirit.

'We've already shown the ads once,' he directed at Roy, 'and everyone was very impressed. You looked good, Roy. Really good. I don't know what you were worried about. Have you seen them, Kate?'

'No, but I'd love to.'

Roy shot her a sharp look, but Kate blithely ignored him. 'Lead me to the television set.'

'Another viewing coming up,' Ned said, and spun his wheelchair around as if it was balanced on a penny, Marla having to dart out of his way.

'Truly, Ned,' she grumbled. 'Must you practise your basketball moves on my foot? Come on, Kate, or we'll be left behind. Roy, get us both a drink, will you?'

Ned was right. Roy looked good. More than good. In fact, he looked so incredibly sexy as he went through his paces in those ads that she could well imagine women lining up for miles to join Body Beautiful gyms all over Sydney, in the hope of meeting *the* body beautiful in the flesh. As for his voice. She hadn't realised before how sensual his voice was, deep and slightly gravelly. It sent tickles down her spine when he looked into the camera's eye and said, 'A fit body is a beautiful body. Come on in to one of our gyms and start being beautiful today.'

'Come on, Kate,' Ned said after they'd finished. 'Give us your honest opinion. They're good, aren't they?'

'You'll have to hire more staff just to answer the phone,' she agreed warmly.

'See, Roy? What did I tell you?'

'You did look good, Roy,' Marla praised.

'He certainly did . . .'

They all swivelled round at this new voice, which belonged to a striking blonde. Peroxide hair, darkly made-up eyes and a scarlet mouth sat upon a well toned yet voluptuous figure, eye-poppingly displayed in a shiny black catsuit.

'Don't you recognise me, Roy?' she purred. 'It's Celia . . . Celia Huntington.'

All eyes moved to Roy, who was looking at the blonde with a wry smile spreading across his face.

'Celia Huntington,' he repeated. 'Well, I never. What on earth are you doing here?'

'I'm a freelance journo these days, specialising in articles for several of the sport magazines. As you know . . .' a sexy smile showed pearly white teeth '. . . I've always been partial to sport.'

'And sportsmen,' Roy added with a darkly amused chuckle.

'Aren't you going to introduce us to your friend, Roy?' Marla said, perhaps noting Kate's frozen stillness at her side.

Kate was unable to say a word while the introductions were made, especially when Roy made no reference to Kate herself being anyone special to him. She was just 'a friend'.

'Could I have a word with you in private, Roy?' Celia asked with another of those sexy smiles. 'I have an idea for an article on The Body Beautiful I'd like to discuss with you.'

'Well, I suppose I can't pass up the opportunity for some free advertising. Look after the ladies, Ned, till I get back.'

Kate watched, dismayed and jealous, as Roy allowed himself to be drawn away. She was falling into the deepest depression when Ned put a hand on her arm.

'Don't go worrying about that tramp,' Ned reassured kindly. 'I recognise the name. She was at university with Roy years ago, a member of the hockey team, if I recall rightly. Roy was quite taken with her till he discovered her main goal that year was to sleep with the entire football team. Apparently he was pretty cut up about it at the time—and I do think the experience might have contributed to the way he treated women for quite a few years—but that's all in the past. Now that he's met someone decent and nice like you, he won't be getting mixed up with tarty blonde bimbos like that any more, will he, Marla?'

Marla didn't look quite so sure. 'What? Oh—er—no, of course not. But perhaps you shouldn't let Celia monopolise Roy for too long, Ned. There are plenty of other media people here wanting interviews as well.'

They all looked over to where Celia had enticed Roy into a very private corner. Kate stiffened when the blonde put her hand on Roy's chest, reaching up to whisper something in his ear. Roy tipped back his head and laughed, the sound stabbing into Kate's heart. When she looked away and met Marla's sympathetic gaze, she felt almost ill.

She knows, came the crushing realisation. Knows what kind of man he is, knows I'm nothing but a temporary diversion, as all women are temporary diversions in his mind. At this very moment he's probably setting up a date with that disgusting creature, that stunningly beautiful, incredibly sexy, but still disgusting creature!

Ned's charging across the room in his wheelchair, intent on breaking up the cosy little twosome, only served to underline Roy's friends' knowledge of his character. Kate was touched that they cared about her feelings, but she knew their actions were futile. Roy would do what he was going to do, regardless. Kate had foreseen this eventuality. What she hadn't anticipated was having to see it happen right under her nose, or the depth of her despair when it did.

'Don't jump to conclusions,' Marla whispered.

Kate blinked and saw concern had replaced the pity.

'Roy just doesn't know how to be rude to people,' Ned's wife went on. 'It doesn't mean anything, his laughing and joking like that. Roy likes to have a good time, likes to be happy. You know about his father, don't you?'

Kate nodded, bewildered over what Roy's father had to do with his flirting with another woman in front of her.

'Well, his father being ill all those years took a big toll on Roy, but he never showed it. His way of coping was to live it up whenever he could. Sure, there were plenty of women and parties, but none of them meant anything.'

'I realise that,' Kate said bitterly. 'Women will never mean anything to Roy. They're just rest and recreation to him. He probably changes them as often as his underwear.'

'He did. Once. But he's changed since his father died. Maybe he's looking to settle down. You're certainly different from any girl he's ever taken out.'

'You mean because I'm older and not good-looking,' Kate bit out. 'Oh, please don't say things just to make me feel better,' she raced on when Marla tried to interrupt. 'I knew what I was getting into when I started seeing Roy. I've amused him, you see, simply because I *am* different. But he doesn't want to settle down with me any more than he wants to settle down with that blonde bombshell. But if I'm any judge, Miss Celia Huntington will be reauditioning for her old role before the week is out.'

'I don't agree,' Marla argued. 'Roy would never go back to her. Not when he could have a woman like you.'

'That's sweet of you, but I don't buy it.'

'Don't sell yourself so short, Kate. And you *are* good-looking, by the way.'

Kate laughed, but it wasn't a happy laugh.

'No, I mean it. I was so glad to see Roy with someone like you. True, you are older than Roy's usual date, and yes, his past girls were all stunners who no doubt knew their way around a bedroom, but honestly, talk about dumb! Roy's a smart man, and next year he'll be thirty. There comes a time when dumb, no matter how beautiful, is boring!'

Kate shook her head, thinking to herself that *she* was the one who was dumb, her love for Roy making her grab at straws where he was concerned. How could she measure up against a gorgeous blonde with all the tricks of the trade? Certainly not for long. Suddenly, she felt old and plain and stupid. Roy had just been playing a game with her, giving himself a change from his usual sexual fare. She was bread and butter pudding instead of caviare, a rusty old T-model Ford instead of a well oiled Cadillac.

'How's it going, lover?'

A pale-faced Kate whirled to see a smiling Roy standing there. Suddenly, she wanted to slap him.

Instead, she smiled stiffly and made some innocuous comment.

'I have to go and give some more interviews,' he continued blithely. 'Can't leave it all to Ned. Then I'm having some publicity photographs taken. You all right here with Marla?'

'Sure.'

'I'll try to be quick.'

'Take your time.'

He frowned at her. 'You sure you're all right?'

'Couldn't be better.'

When he shrugged and strode off, she turned to Marla and said, 'Let's have another drink. I think I need it.'

Roy was as good as his word. He wasn't all that long. But Kate noticed how Celia hung around him like a bad smell whenever she could. The final straw came when Roy returned to herself and Marla, and Celia deliberately called out to him that she was going home but would ring him first thing Monday morning.

'Fine,' he replied, then turned back to them without so much as a hint of discomfort in his demeanour.

'Ned's given me permission to go, Marla,' he said. 'He's over there somewhere giving another interview. The man's inexhaustible. I don't know how you keep up with him.'

'I don't try.'

'Well, Kate? Ready to leave? Say goodnight to Marla. Look after that crazy husband of yours, sweetie.' And he kissed Marla on the cheek.

'Will do, Roy. And you look after this lovely girl of yours.'

'Naturally.'

Kate flinched when he gave her a hug.

'Goodnight, Marla,' she said. 'Nice meeting you.'
'And you.'

Kate made her decision as Roy walked her down to the Mercedes. She had to stop this before it broke her heart beyond repair.

'Roy,' she said shakily when he had opened the passenger door and had walked round to the driver's side, 'I...I think you'd better take me home.'

He stared at her across the bonnet of the car. 'Why?'

'Because...'

'Because why?' he repeated in a low, deadly voice.

'Because I want to go home.'

'Get in this car, Kate. We'll talk about this at my place.'

Kate knew once she was at his place she would not have the courage to follow through with her decision. 'No, Roy. If you won't drive me home I'll catch a taxi.'

Just then she saw one coming down the road in the distance. Sensing that she would only have this one opportunity of escape, she dashed across the car park and on to the pavement, waving frantically. The taxi saw her and stopped and she went to run across the road.

'Kate! Watch out!' Roy screamed.

She had not seen the dark blue sedan coming the other way, but Roy's shouted warning sent her jumping backwards. The car sped past the very spot she'd been about to walk into with a millionth of a second's grace.

What happened then was hazy. She turned and staggered back into the gutter, after-shock making the blood suddenly drain from her face. She might have

fainted if Roy hadn't gathered her hard into his arms
and against his rock-like chest.

'Oh, Kate . . . Kate,' he cried, his voice trembling.
'You could have been killed!'

'Hey!' the taxi driver called out. 'Is she all right,
mate?'

'Yes, I think so,' Roy called back. 'Thanks, but she
won't need you now.'

'No sweat. 'Night.'

'I . . . I didn't see it,' Kate cried into Roy's chest.

'I did. And I saw a hell I had never dreamt existed.'
He held her away from him, staring down at her with
haunted eyes. 'I refuse to wait for you to really fall
in love with me. I'm going to speak now and to hell
with patience. I love you, Kate. And I want you to
marry me, as soon as possible. Say you will, my
darling. Say you will!'

She gaped up at him, disbelieving. But finally she
was able to take in his white face, his quivering hands,
his quite uncharacteristic desperation. And she knew
he meant every word. Or thought he did.

Swallowing down the sense of unreality, trying to
choke down the upsurge of sheer joy, she looked up
at him and asked what had to be asked. 'What . . . what
about you and Celia?'

'Me and Celia? What in hell are you talking about?
I wouldn't touch that slut with a barge-pole! Oh, I
see . . . she said she was going to call me. That's for
an interview, which I will turn down. I just didn't
want her putting on a turn tonight. But me and *Celia*?'
He shuddered violently, as though only then realising
what Kate had been envisaging. 'My God, what a re-
volting thought. How could you even think it?'

'I . . . I guess I was blindly jealous,' she confessed.

He smiled. 'I like the sound of that. So! Now I've answered your irrational and might I say not very flattering question, what's your answer? Will you marry me?' His eyes filled suddenly with the most appealing vulnerability. 'Don't say no, for pity's sake. I love you, Kate. I need you...'

Kate felt her heart swell at the realisation that she was indeed the special woman he'd been waiting for. She'd been too blinded by her own inferiority complex before to see it. But now she did. She saw it all. His persistence. His passion. His very real and very wonderful love. Her heart filled to overflowing.

Taking a deep breath, she said the words she'd thought she would never have a chance to say. 'And I love and need you, Roy. Yes. I will marry you.'

Now it was his turn to look stunned. But then he whooped with delight and swung her round before putting her down and kissing her soundly.

'Hey, what's the celebration?' Ned called out from where Marla was wheeling him down the ramp.

'The lady said yes!' Roy announced proudly, and led Kate back over to the bottom of the ramp.

'Yeah, but yes to what?' Ned asked.

'Marriage, mate. Marriage.'

'You're not serious.' Ned frowned. 'You've only known each other a couple of weeks.'

Roy looked startled. 'Have we? Hell, it feels a lot longer than that.'

'Actually, Roy,' Kate said softly, 'it's shorter. It's one week, five days and...' she glanced at her watch '...seventeen hours.'

Ned and Marla looked at each other and nodded. 'She loves him,' they said in dry unison.

'And I love her,' Roy insisted stubbornly. 'Hell, I'm crazy about her!'

'Well, what are you waiting for, then?' Ned flung at him. 'Grab the lady before some other lucky chap does.'

'But you just said——'

'Oh, for pity's sake take me home, Marla,' Ned grumbled. 'The man's too besotted to know what I said. As if I'd ever tell anyone to wait. Remember when we met, darling? I asked you to marry me that very first night, didn't I?'

'Yes, sweetheart. But that was because you wanted to take me to bed and you thought that was a good enough line.'

'It's still a good line.' He darted Roy a savage look. 'You're not just throwing Kate a line to get her into bed, are you?'

Both Roy and Kate burst out laughing.

'Stupid man,' Marla muttered, and wheeled him away.

'You're not just marrying me to get me into bed, Kate, are you?' Roy asked quite seriously as soon as they were out of earshot.

'Would I do that?' Kate asked with wide, innocent eyes. 'Come on, darling, let's go home...to bed.' And she swanned off towards the Mercedes, the most deliciously satisfied smile on her face.

EPILOGUE

'I'M GOING to miss you.'

Kate looked up from where she was cleaning out her desk. 'I'll miss you too, Estelle.'

'I wish I could get up to Armidale for the wedding. The other girls were green with envy when I got an invitation. But it's my mum's fiftieth birthday that weekend and she'd kill me if I missed it.'

'I understand entirely, Estelle. My mother would do exactly the same.'

'How does your mum feel about your marrying someone like Roy? I'll bet she was surprised. I certainly was. Never thought Roy Fitzsimmons would marry *any* woman, let alone my boss!'

Kate smiled as she fingered her beautiful engagement ring. 'Actually, Mum wasn't as surprised as I thought she'd be. Mothers are smarter than we give them credit for, I think.'

'Yeah, my mom always knows when I've been up to no good.' Estelle sighed theatrically. 'I wonder who they're going to get to replace you. It'll probably be some crabby old bitch who'll never give me an early mark. Are you sure you won't need a secretary over at The Body Beautiful?'

Kate laughed. '*I'm* going to be the secretary.' Plus the accountant and the trouble-shooter and the general dogsbody, she added wryly to herself.

When Roy had casually mentioned to her one night that they hadn't enough funds to employ a proper company secretary as yet, she'd taken the hint and looked at the books. Knowing Roy's paranoia for financial security, she realised a professional hand was urgently needed before they got themselves into financial difficulties, so she had offered her services in exchange for a small salary and a share in the company's profits. Both Roy and Ned had jumped at the chance to have someone with her qualifications looking after their investment.

'I heard from quarters on high,' Kate resumed while continuing to empty her drawers, 'that this position has been filled by a man.'

Estelle brightened immediately. 'A man?'

'Yes, a Mr Robinson, from the Melbourne branch.'

'From the Melbourne branch?'

'That's right. I met him once. He's quite young, and good-looking and, most importantly, unattached.'

'No kidding!'

'Would I kid?'

'I wouldn't put it past you. I wouldn't put *anything* past you these days, Kate Reynolds!'

Kate laughed. 'I'll take that as a compliment. Now go and empty this waste-paper basket into the incinerator. It's chocka, and I've still a couple of drawers to go yet. And a cup of coffee wouldn't go astray. Thanks a million.'

Estelle picked up the basket and breezed out, giving Kate a few minutes' privacy. Which was as well, since she'd just opened the drawer into which she'd stuffed the poster of Roy all those weeks ago.

Seeing it brought a rueful smile to her face. If Roy knew she had this picture of him in her possession he would be so embarrassed. Truly, any other man would be proud of having such a body. Yet in some ways he found it vaguely disconcerting, perhaps because he hated it when women didn't look beyond the physical to the man beneath. Which had happened. Both with Celia, and lots of other women, she gathered.

Roy had even thought that of Kate herself for a while, and she had to concede that she might have given that impression. But that was before she knew he loved her as she loved him, and before she learnt what real love meant. It did not rely on looks, or superficial attractions. It was far, far deeper than that. Kate knew she would love Roy long after he'd lost his looks and his muscles.

Kate sighed softly, and unrolled the poster to have one last look before she consigned it to the pile of rubbish.

Tears filled her eyes as she stared down at the man she loved, seeing again the vulnerability in those beautiful blue eyes, the secret loneliness. There he was, looking as if he should have the world in the palm of his hand, but behind that arrogant macho physique had lain a man just wanting to be loved, aching to be cared for and nurtured as he'd never been nurtured.

Not that he wanted to be mothered. He was far too independent for that. But he did want someone to share his life with to the nth degree, someone to create a family with. Already they had talked of babies. In fact, a few weeks back, they'd decided not to do anything to prevent a pregnancy, and already Kate had her suspicions.

A baby...

She smiled and dashed away her tears. This was no time for crying. This was a time of joy, of looking forward, never backward.

Abruptly she scrunched the poster up, compressing it into a little ball. Hearing someone come into the room, she looked up, expecting it be Estelle. Roy stood there, dressed in baggy blue jeans and an old Sloppy Joe, disreputable-looking trainers on his feet. She had a sneaky suspicion that he chose to wear ghastly old clothes sometimes in a vain attempt to play down his physical appeal.

Kate's smile was gently wry as she dropped the ball of paper back into a drawer. Silly man. He would look great in anything. 'Now what are you doing here at this time of day?' she asked teasingly.

'Came to see my girl, make sure she's all right.'

'And why wouldn't I be all right?'

'You looked a little pale this morning.'

She laughed. 'I look pale every morning. That's my normal colour without make-up. Pale.'

'I thought you were extra pale this morning,' he insisted, looking at her with a question in his eyes.

A lump came to her throat. He knows, she thought. I haven't said anything yet, but he knows.

'Roy,' she said with a catch in her voice, 'it's too early to tell. I'm only five days late and——'

Any protest died in her throat when he strode forward and placed a box on her desk. 'Just bought it from the chemist downstairs,' he said firmly. 'They said it worked at two weeks.'

She stared down at the pregnancy-testing kit then up at Roy's serious face. Gulping, she picked up the box and headed for the washroom. When she came out, she was indeed pale.

'It . . . it turned blue,' she croaked.

Roy took an anxious step towards her. 'And?'

'That's positive. We're ... we're going to have a baby.'

Whooping with elation, Roy swooped on her, swinging her round before setting her back on to her shaky feet and kissing her soundly. He was still kissing her when Estelle returned with the empty waste-paper basket and a mug of steaming coffee. She deposited both without the kissing couple even noticing her presence.

'Aah ... true love,' the secretary murmured wistfully, and, showing decorum for the first time in her life, she quietly left the room, shutting the door behind her.